I0772400

Red Black Rainbow

or

The Dogs, The Dandelion, and the Blue-Eyed Rat

A Modern Morality Play

By

James Alejandro-Sueling-Loons

For Judith and Bert,
the daily rainbows of my week

For Avery,
The rainbow of my life

and for my Mother,
who gave me the heart and mind
to understand the difference I could make
and the courage to set out and do it.
If Heaven is real, I hope she sees the difference her son made.

The author begs you to not continue.

Deny the insatiable curiosity you feel looking at the menu
included to aid in your digestion should you decide
to swallow the lump in your throat and go any further.
Cast this book away and never think of it again.

Please know that I was the first to wretch and heave
and fight back the bile as I read what my hand had written.
I lost the battle twice.

All warnings aside, it is a Prix Fixe worth dining on
and rolling around in your mouth.
After all, the gentle swirl of a tongue is the only way
a rainbow of flavors can combine and emerge
in even the gamiest meat.

Whoever you may be, consider this your last chance to get out now and never wonder about what happened on 116th Street in Harlem between a little old lady and her skinhead neighbors.

For those of you brave enough to try and beat the devil, you'll come out changed.

A simple idea gnawed at my mind throughout the pandemic and Summer following the murders of Breonna Taylor and George Floyd with the 2020 election looming; *what if this had been during the Obama years?*

This story is part fact, part fiction, part brief but historical account of racism throughout the United States wrapped in a Morality Play.

Though the Dog Whistlers are an amalgam of Ultra Supremacist Groups across America, the individuals are based only on the horrors of my mind.

Rainbow, David, Lisa and anyone else in the main story are also imagined, but I know many people just like all of them and hope you do as well. They're the only way to get a world full of bad dogs to heel.

You may find this story unsettling, uncomfortable, and at moments may want to crawl out of your skin. That is the American Experience no matter which way you cut it.

Interludes appearing in this font are my own summations of modern American violence against the Human Race through the targeting of Black individuals. While they inform the journey, they are not part of the entirely fictitious.

Chapter One

7/1/2008: The Invisible Thread

"Will remember you when I am smoking those cigarettes.
Well bye, bye."
~Percy Kingsley in a letter to a Miss Hanley
following the Battle of Ypres

It wasn't premeditated then, he had actually been the one who was supposed to get hurt.

He didn't know what *red laces* meant then.

He didn't know these three guys buying him a shot after shot of Jäegermeister weren't planning on a fourway.

He didn't know there were so many of them two years ago, but he did now.

And *none* of it was an accident anymore.

So when he saw Apartment 7 on Craigslist, he knew it was time to put it to bed for good.

Chapter 2

4/20/2007: 14words.com

Matthew got out of the car and double clicked the alarm while he prepared to con what seemed like a nice enough White couple into signing a lease on one of four shithole properties Lisa had left him in the divorce.

The *empty since she bought it,* bar at number 45 and three rent stabilized buildings down the street, all mostly city program occupied. Completely untouchable and perpetually devaluing every time a junkie overshot or like in Apartment 7 in the one on the right, was shot. Chest to barrel with a shotgun pressed against the living room floor over an underweight and overcut bag of dope.

It had been his and Lisa's first crisis and crash course in being landlords, not their last, *just the worst,* and the one on Matthew's mind as he saw a Mercedes Benz that made his Saab look like shit stop outside the vacant space. His prospective tenants getting out of the car in unison snapped him back from that first morning to now.

He *needed* this lease to happen.
"Hi, are you Gunnar and Evangeline?"
"Yes, we are, and that makes you Matthew?"
He was a large man, but not fat. *Sturdy? Solid?*
Matthew didn't know the right word for someone who looked like what his own father would have called an "*Ubermensch*" but he felt like calling a 6'4 Blond, Blue-Eyed, prospective

tenant an Ubermensch outside a dilapidated bar in Harlem
might be too close to inappropriate for comfort.

And for as perfectly in shape as he was, his wife made
him look like a thumb.

She was tall with a coil of perfectly braided blonde hair
wound into a tight bun that pulled her already sharp features
into a face that looked like it was carved from alabaster and
painted perfectly with subtle and delicate blush, mascara, and a
shade of red lipstick he had never seen.

As Matthew pulled the ring of keys from his bag and
searched for the one numbered 45 he found a new thought,
*what did this nice White couple want with a bar in a
neighborhood that had so clearly failed to gentrify? Were they
hoping to get in when things were cheap and hope for a bounce
back?*
They were a few years late on that.

The only open storefronts on the block were an old and run
down bodega that sold near-expired food and Chopped Cheese
on toasted moldy bread to the crackheads, junkies and corner
boys who kept them supplied; and the barbecue joint that had
somehow survived nearly 100 years next door to the bar he was
hoping to rent and was run by a woman named Rainbow who
had to be nearly 70 and had almost no patience for White
People.
And who could blame her?
From what Matthew had gleaned, her dad had been murdered
in the 1960s during the Civil Rights Movement.

"Have you been looking at potential spaces for very long?" Matthew tried to sound like the Saab dealership hadn't called to remind him that this month's payment was already 19 days late as he had been waiting for them to arrive.

"Not as long as it took us to find a spot in Chicago," Gunnar replied, smiling first at the narrow L-shaped hallway behind the porthole front door and then the Walnut Bar running the length of one wall and the enormous parquet dance floor it faced, all patinated by 100 years of nights filled with smoke and noise.

"What and where in Chicago? I've been a Northsider since birth. My ex-wife is what brought me to Manhattan," Matthew said as he felt the mood ease.

"I know you'd never expect it, but my wife is a huge fan of Punk Rock and Dive Bars," Gunnar said and squeezed Evangeline gently.

"And dogs," Evangeline added and squeezed in return.

"Right. And dogs. She wants to open a bar here that has good tunes, cheap beer...and dogs. Sure it's a novel idea but you know how people are with their pets now. Evangeline calls our German Shepherd our *furbaby*, yes, the term freaks me out, but he truly is spoiled. She cooks him a steak for dinner nightly. Rare and pink." Gunnar was laying it on thick but Matthew knew this was a done deal the minute Evangeline pushed open the door at the back and sunlight came pouring in through the unkempt yard that he had intentionally neglected to mention in the listing.

A true Manhattan surprise for only the *truly* interested.

"Wir könnten einen Biergarten haben!" Evangeline shouted as the tall grass and weeds enveloped her legs while she wandered further outside.

"All I got from that was Biergarten..." Matthew said while watching Gunnar investigate what was behind the bar.

"Oh, it's German. It's actually how we knew we were meant to be together. Both of our parents are from the Fatherland and still barely speak English. When she gets excited like this she slips into it and doesn't realize," Gunnar explained while lazily opening cupboards and knocking on pipes.

The smell of barbecue had begun wafting in ever since Evangeline had opened the door to the "Biergarten."

What Matthew still couldn't figure out was *why Harlem?* Sure the rent was cheap, but no cheaper than Alphabet City or Bushwick. If hipster punk rockers with dogs was what Gunnar and Evangeline were hoping to find, 116th Street was not the place. At best, a few obtuse Columbia students might brave the journey across Morningside Park, but he didn't see drunken 2 a.m. stumble homes through the place where White women joggers went to get raped and murdered becoming a permanent thing.

And then Gunnar said something that stopped Matthew's thought train in its tracks.

"I know the rent is listed at $5,000 per month but if we prepaid for 12 months could you do 55k in cash?"

Matthew had to consciously not raise an eyebrow.
He had to know *why* they wanted *this* space.

But he knew that $55,000 in cash meant he wouldn't necessarily have to tell Lisa or the lawyers.

She may have left him with shit properties but her lawyer had known that the alimony payments would never be late thanks to the city housing units down the block. It had been a final *fuck you* that made the next thing Matthew said come out as easily as when Lisa had told him she wanted a divorce.

"I can handle that if you can tell me just one thing," Matthew started, "why *this* bar? There are other empty bars in more stable parts of the city."

"But other bars don't have *this* Wunderschön Biergarten!" Evangeline called from the white afternoon light.

And for some reason the word "*Ubermensch*" returned to Matthew's mind.

**

In the silence of that evening Matthew considered how his luck
had finally changed as he laid the stacks of bundles of cash in a
perfect rectangle over a towel on the table in the apartment he
had moved into when Lisa told him to get out for the last time.
It was all there.
Real as far as his bill markers and holding a few of the
Benjamins up to the light could tell.

The offer had been more than Matthew had expected but
when Gunnar had popped the trunk on the Benz and told
Matthew to take it to his car and count it, his greed put his
humanity and conscience on ice.
The moment he got in the Saab and unzipped the duffel, he
took a breath, wound the three keys to the bar off the ring,
peeled a few bills off the top of the pile without looking down,
rezipped the bag, pushed it under the seat between his legs, and
got back out. Double beeping the lock and alarm as he did.

"Gunnar, Evangeline, what say we pop into Rainbow's
and have some barbecue to celebrate you having the only punk
dive bar with dogs and a beer garden in Harlem," Matthew
said, the keys glinting in the sunlight as he walked toward the
door of number 47.
"It's mostly 20s and 50s. The bank might ask where it
all came from, I'll remind you that we own a bar in Chicago.
We also have houses in Florida, Texas, Oklahoma, and in our
hometown, Portland. Evangeline's Dad's family runs a coffee

shop and my great granddad on my mother's side was mayor in the 1920s," Gunnar shared as he and Evangeline began to follow Matthew toward the door.

"I thought you said your parents were German?" Matthew casually asked as he pushed the door open and the smell of roasted meat wafted out.

"They are. We are one-hundred percent German blood going back eight generations on my side and eight on his," Evangeline said, making her lips pucker and fall as she said *100% German*. It was mesmerizing to watch her mouth move, to watch her move, *and then it happened.*

He wouldn't have believed it if he hadn't seen it happen right in front of him.

"Hello, Matthew, nice to see you," Rainbow lied while sizing up the two Aryans who had followed him in. "Are these friends of yours? *Come for some of the finest hot links and flats this side of the Mason-Dixon?*" she couldn't help but barb them.

She knew racists when she saw them and judging by the German car parked outside she hadn't remembered feeling this certain since the day her father had been beaten to death.

The day Malcolm X was shot.

The day Temple 7 had been bombed.

The day she had met her first bonafide Aryan Men and everything that had happened between them between dusk and the rooster on the roof crowing at dawn.

"These are actually your new neighbors. Evangeline and Gunnar. They just rented the bar next door for at least the next year. A dog bar with a beer garden out back," Matthew was practically bragging.

They hadn't always had the friendliest relationship, Lisa had been a capital B Bitch to Rainbow since the morning they met.

The morning after the crisis in apartment 7.
While Lisa was talking to the police in the street as the coroner came in and yellow tape went up around the block, Rainbow had been out on her balcony watching like a queen in her tower, and then for seemingly no reason had yelled down, "did you even know the dead guy in 7's name?"
That had set Lisa entirely off.

"Someone is dead and you're still mad that a White Couple bought the building next door? It's barely 7am and you're *already* making this *horrific* tragedy about Gentrification," Lisa had said to the sky without looking up. The police had finally finished around 11am, the same time that the White vinyl shade pulled up and the door to #47 popped and propped open for the day.

Lisa had walked, no, *marched*, into Rainbow's Barbecue and demanded, "Who was that woman upstairs this morning? *Someone was murdered*. Shot point blank with a shotgun to the chest and she—" Lisa was abruptly interrupted.

"Shot point blank with a shotgun? Are you talking about Minister Malcolm X?" Rainbow knew where this was going and planned on using this White Lady's righteous indignation against her and then get on with her day.

"*What?* No. *The man in apartment 7* who was killed early this morning," Lisa shot back with as much venom as she could muster.

"And I'll ask you again, *what was his name?*"
That was how Rainbow and Lisa and Matthew had met, and now the memory of that morning seemed like friendship compared to what happened just after Rainbow met Gunnar and Evangeline.

**

"I'm not a member of the Nation, but I do my best to only serve cuts of meat that Allah would allow if he tasted them," Rainbow had joked as she disappeared into the back and Matthew went for the booth by the window.

"I'm sorry Matthew, we won't be eating *here*." Gunnar had said.

"Is something wrong? Rainbow has a perfect health inspection report, the best dry rub in the city, and you're neighbors now," Matthew laid it on because he knew what Rainbow not liking you meant.
It wouldn't matter how many Columbia kids did or didn't come.
Once she told people that you were a Dick, it stuck.
That's the thing about lifelong neighborhood fixtures, they have rule of the roost.

"Nothing is wrong, we knew there'd be monkeys in the zoo. This *is* Harlem after all," Evangeline said as she began digging mindlessly in her purse.

Matthew gawped.

"There's no polite way to say this, but some things just are what they are and my Vater taught me, 'kein schwarzes Essen'."

"I'm sorry but I took French in high school," Matthew thought he understood but hoped he was wrong.

"We don't eat food made by Coons." Evangeline's lips no longer looked mesmerizing, they looked evil.

"Well, I don't know what to say to that," Matthew had said thinking it would all end up being some sick prank.

Evangeline looked at the photos on the wall, the perfectly spotless linoleum floor, and then began to say, "We don't eat food made by *nigg-*"

And that's when things went from bad to worse.
While Evangeline was still in the double g's of her slur Rainbow came back out.

"*That's* enough. I knew you two were assholes the minute I saw you get out of your fine German automobile. I don't know *what* you're doing or why you're *here*, but I do know that you can keep your scrawny Lily-White backside out of my Barbecue. Now. You two. Get out. *Now.*"

Matthew thought about all of it from that first morning with the guy in apartment 7 to that conversation he folded the towel over the money and put it back in the duffel.
This had been one helluva day.

Nobody got shot, but for the first time in his life Matthew had heard a White person, a *White Woman* at that, use the N-word.

And that same woman's husband had given him over $50,000 in cash on a handshake lease.

His greed had cooled, but not enough to change his mind. Just enough to feel rich and guilty. He would have run after them to give it back but Rainbow had made him stay. She had asked what the fuck he was thinking and he did the only thing he could think of, *he lied*.

He told her Lisa had been the one to do all the screenings and paperwork, he had just been the guy handing over keys and *thought* he was introducing the new neighbors.

Because what was Rainbow going to do? Call Lisa? Did she even have her number? Would she even pick up if she did?

He left all the bills he had blindly pulled from the duffel on the table when he left Rainbow's; three 50s. She had picked them up, then realizing where they had probably come from, she dropped them in the trash.

She pulled out her black book and dialed a number.
It rang twice and then she said, "Hello, Lisa?"

Chapter Three

2/21/1965: Keds, Killing, Knocking

"Brothers! Brothers! Please! This is a house of Peace!"
~Malcolm X at The Audubon Ballroom

Rainbow had lived in the apartment above the restaurant since the day her parents brought her home from the hospital one August morning in 1944. Her father had made the best barbecue in Harlem since his own father had taught him how to thread the casing tube onto the grinder when he was seven years old.

But as Rainbow sat next to the bed, looking at the half her mother had occupied until three years ago when brain cancer had eaten all her Gray Meat up in a matter of months and mouthfuls of morphine; she realized that soon both halves of this bed would be permanently empty, and everything about this place, from the oldest, dustiest box in the basement to the freshest piece of produce in the walk in, *all of it,* would be entirely hers to deal with.

"Daddy, you hold on now. This is bad, but you're strong and without you, I don't know how I'll survive," she said while choking back tears and wiping the blood off his face. Being delicate around the gash on his forehead and the black and blue softball that used to be his left eye.

Nobody had expected the hopeful words that Malcolm X had shared this morning to turn into an afternoon of anger or this dark night of violence and fear when Rainbow had gone to the Audubon Ballroom this morning, dressed presentable but in shoes she could run in if anything had gone wrong.
She thought wearing White Keds with her dress made her look like a nurse, but now after running from 165 to 116 while cops let go of the dog leashes and opened the fire hoses just enough to create a jet of freezing water strong enough to break skin and

send you ass over tea kettle down the block before you even had time to realize you were wet; she'd never been more grateful for what her daddy had always called Peds.

"Are some of them followers of Elijah Muhammad?" a reporter for ABC News was asking the chief of police.

"Yes, they come from all the various walks of life and are connected with different organizations and we are questioning anyone and everyone who might be of help," the chief replied as sirens rang out in the darkness behind him.

"Chief, does this indicate to you that this is just the first, the beginning, of a series of incidents between these two rival groups?"

"No, I wouldn't comment on that at all."
And with that Rainbow clicked off the black and white RCA in her parents bedroom and watched as the image of Chief Murphy collapsed into a blip of white light and disappeared into the crackling sound of the TV tube powering off and cooling down.

It had only been a little over six months since that White bastard Patrick Lynch had set Harlem on fire for six nights when he got James Powell killed at the hand of officer Gilligan.

Rainbow hadn't been there but a boy she knew had been. Cliff Harris. He had told the NYPD that James had given him and their other friend Karl Dudley each a knife to hold onto until he asked for them back. Cliff had stated that he didn't pull the knife he had been given out of his bag. He had refused but Carl had acquiesced after Patrick Lynch turned his hose on the group of kids and yelled repeatedly "DIRTY NIGGERS! I'll wash you clean!"

According to some of the other kids that was when the three boys began picking up rocks and trash and hurling it at Mr. Lynch.

That was when he turned heel and ran into his building and James Powell followed, knife in hand. Everyone said they heard shouting and things breaking and that was when officer Gilligan had come around the corner and the whole situation went to hell.

"I'm a police Lieutenant, come out and drop it!" Gilligan yelled as the group of kids became a huddled mass on the sidewalk.

Officer Gilligan filed a report saying that James Powell had come out brandishing the knife. Gilligan had fired a warning shot that broke a window when Powell swung the first time. That he had shot him in his arm when he raised the knife again and that he shot him in the gut; this bullet exiting his back and sending him down the front steps into a pool of blood where he died.

One shot through and through.

One bullet, the second, shot through his forearm, through his main artery and lodged itself in his lungs.

The coroner noted in the autopsy report that James Powell could have survived if the ambulance had arrived on time.

Those six nights of chaos last summer had been a sea change in the social dynamics of Harlem. The NYPD had gone from a phantom threat to undeniable murderers in three shots and sloppy policing.

Daddy sat downstairs for those six nights, shade to the window pulled, every light turned off, listening to the sounds of running and screaming and breaking glass.
He told Rainbow to stay upstairs no matter what she heard happening. But in all six nights nobody had tried to mess with the restaurant or daddy.

The neighborhood calmed down over the course of a week but not before the protest outside the school in Yorkville where 300 people led by CORE, the Congress of Racial Equality, joined in a chant of "stop killer cops" and "we want legal protection" and "end police brutality".

Not before that almost 100 degree weekend where James Powell's funeral had to be managed and controlled *by* the NYPD.

And not before Reverend Dukes had organized the March on the 28th Precinct backed by Black Nationalists, Edward Mills and James Lawson.

Following the march to 123rd Street Inspector Pendergast had agreed to a private meeting with the men. By the time it was over, the crowd decided they'd had enough waiting for Justice and took to the roofs of buildings and began lobbing any loose bricks, tiles, pieces of rubble, and glass they could find.

With the police below, somewhere around 9:00 PM the first officer was hit. A direct hit with a glass bottle to the face of officer Doris. By 10:00 PM over 1,000 Harlemites had taken over 125th Street and 7th Avenue.
As the NYPD yelled for everyone to go home, the crowd yelled back "we *are* home baby!"
Throughout that night the police broke the protest into smaller groups and pushed them further and further into the neighborhoods of Harlem. Some were pushed to Columbia, some toward the East Side, but at 8:00 AM the next morning Rainbow saw the final group send the exhausted cops fleeing past the restaurant and up and around the block toward the precinct.

The news was slow to report the entirety of that first night but one person had died. The tactical police force had, at some point, turned their 38s toward the rooftops in the dark and fired randomly.

19 people had gone to the hospital for their injuries but so had a dozen cops.

Victory felt small, but knowing the NYPD wouldn't feel emboldened enough to shoot and kill black boys in the ninth grade for a while had to go in the win column.

Rainbow told daddy that she was going to check on a few friends that afternoon and it hadn't entirely been a lie. It just happened that one of the younger girls she knew, Judith, had told her to meet on a corner and had dragged her to the CORE rally discussing the night before and what the plan was for the next.

Judith had waited patiently for any of the adults to suggest an action plan that would lead to permanent change but when the end of the meeting arrived, no solution in sight, Judith had put her hand on Rainbow's shoulder and stepped up onto her chair before yelling,

"We got a Civil Rights Bill and along with the Bill we got Barry Goldwater and a dead Black boy. This shooting of James Powell was *murder*!"

That Sunday every House of worship across Harlem was packed. Every pew full. Men standing at the backs of the rooms and along the edges of the aisles.

Rainbow and her daddy had gone to Temple 7. Not because they were of the faith or because Malcolm X was there, but because the Temple was on their block; a direct census of their neighborhood.

Minister Malcolm said, "there are probably more armed negroes in Harlem than in any other spot on earth." Just as commissioner Murphy came through the doors with the same statement he had given and delivered personally to every church, temple, and congregation in Harlem."

Minister Malcolm paused to let the Commissioner hand him the letter and had read it silently before handing it back and then looking the commissioner straight in the eye said,

"If people who are armed get involved in this, you can bet they'll really have something on their hands."

That night last summer had been the first time Rainbow remembered not being open for dinner. It had also been the second to last time she heard Malcolm X speak.

Today was the last.

She thought about James Powell and the men on the roofs last summer, she thought about how cold the fire hoses were as she ran from the Audubon to home on icy February sidewalks sliding and skidding as her "Ked-Peds" tried to find purchase with every footfall.
She thought about how someone behind her had yelled "get your hand out of my pocket" before something had started on fire and was thrown.
The chemical smell and smoke as she saw the photo film burning under a chair a few rows ahead.
How Betty had yelled as she ran at those men who rushed the stage.
She thought about that man who pulled a sawed off shotgun from under his folded coat and aimed it at minister Malcolm's chest, how the flash of light and bang of gunfire sent buckshot into the minister's chest and face as his wife Betty wailed "they're killing my husband!"
        Rainbow thought of how that must have been the last thing Malcolm X heard as two more men rushed the stage, standing over him and fired revolvers into his legs and body.
She thought of that nearly 60 block run home she had made, never slowing or looking back.

She thought about last summer, about James Powell and her friend Judith, and how if the death of a little black boy lit her neighborhood on fire for nearly a week; *that this assassination may just burn everything above 110th Street to the ground.*

She had come rushing into the dining room downstairs as her daddy was handing the neighbors across the way a bag of barbecue and he almost dropped it when he saw how dirty her Peds were, how out of breath she was. He told them to just pay tomorrow but to get home *now* as she gulped down two big glasses of water and daddy pulled the shades and cut the music off, there was an enormous boom that shook the silverware and plates and rattled the bell on the door and then everything smelled like smoke and fire and she heard women and children screaming and the sound of rushing feet on the sidewalk outside.
And then she heard banging on the door and a White Man yelling for daddy to open it.

Chapter Four

6/6/2006: Omens, Odins, One Night of Hell

"5 words."
~KWSL

"There are no atheists in foxholes."
~President Eisenhower

David had loved horror movies since he was little. It was the idea that for as dangerous as the people of the world were; aliens, ghosts, or possession by the devil was even scarier than being alone with two strangers on the El.

He had grown up a child of the 1990s. Divorced and inattentive parents, a latchkey kid.

He knew he was gay by the time he was nine and knew that living on a farm with his mom and step-dad wasn't a long term solution by nine and a half.

When he was 12 and too big for Frank, his mom's husband, to beat on him anymore, he was sent to his dad's house on a Reservation in Minnesota.

At 14 he had come out of the closet.

Fed up with the White boys at school shoulder checking him and dumping their lunch trays down his back in the cafeteria.

He had written his dad a letter explaining that he was gay but hoped his dad loved him anyway.

His dad had been waiting when he got home from school that day in 2002. He'd told him to pack enough clothes for a few days and loaded him into the back seat of his Buick LeSabre.

They had driven to the highway and southbound on I-35.

When they stopped at a Flying J outside Ames, David had gone into the filling station and out the back to the line of Semis and gotten in the first truck that felt safe.

A man named Charlie had driven him to Chicago.

To a neighborhood called Boystown and told him to be careful about who he let take him in before handing him all the cash in his wallet and pulling away.

It was $276, and that had been 4 years ago.

He'd slept on benches and in doorways for a week until a social worker had asked if he wanted to go to a diner and talk.

He trusted her. Val, a beautiful Black woman who dedicated herself to saving wayward queer kids. She had kept him out of the system by letting him live on her couch for almost three years until he was old enough to get a lease on a studio of his own.

He had gotten a job at the movie theater down the block and as far as he knew none of his family had ever come looking for him.

As the late screening of the big weekend release let out he saw a group of three punk boys come out of "The Omen" talking about how the original was better but seeing the remake on 6/6/06 was something to brag about.

One was talking about how Julia Stiles was to blame for Damien's identity, "She was married to a Jew, what did she expect," the boy with red laces had said.

"Did you guys like the nanny scene?" David asked as he swept popcorn out of the aisle and into the dustbin.

"Are you talking to us?" red laces had asked back.

"Oh. Yeah, sorry. I got to see it last night but haven't had anyone to talk to about it yet," David sheepishly said without looking up.

One of the other boys whispered something to red laces and they both started giggling,

"Oh...you're looking for *some boys to talk to??*" red laces asked and broke into laughter sending the other two into giggle fits all over again.

"Sorry, I just haven't seen you guys around before and assumed—"

"Assumed what?" asked the shorter of the other two.

"Well, I mean, this *is* Boystown..." David said thinking he misread these boys.

"Oh, well as it happens we were thinking about finding a boy around here to talk to..." red laces said while smirking.

And that was how 20 minutes later three men followed David down the block, up three flights of stairs, and into the third worst night of his life. They had all four crowded into David's shoebox Studio apartment while he changed out of his popcorn scented uniform and into his cutoff shorts and a T-shirt from Madonna's Reinvention tour.

"My adoptive mom Val took me two years ago when the tour stopped here. We're seeing the Confessions tour in a couple weeks," David said as he pulled his shirt over his head. He had learned their names. Red laces was Odin, the shorter of the other two was named Rowan and the tall one was named Cade.

"So you just try to hit on boys at the movies and wear Madonna shirts when you're done?" Cade had asked.

"Sometimes it's a Christina Aguilera shirt," David had joked back.

"David's a Jewish name right?" Rowan had asked casually while opening and closing the drawers in the kitchen.

"Maybe? My mom named me after David from the Bible. You know the story about David and Goliath?" David asked.

"We're into Positive Christianity," Cade replied, "no Old Testament, Hebrew bullshit. Just the belief that the Father was the herald of a new Revelation."

"Oh, well it sounds positive?" David offered.

"It is. We will one day eradicate all darkness and leave only beautiful White light in the world," Rowan said and smirked.

"There's a bar around the corner that doesn't card if you guys want to get a drink." David ended this round of religious posturing as he slipped on his Pro-Ked 69ers and opened the door to the hallway.

When they walked into the bar Cade groaned and asked if it was a gay bar.

"Were you hoping for some punk dive?" David asked.

"Well we only drink German beer and Jägermeister and I don't think most queer bars—" Cade was cut off by David turning and yelling.

"Tony, 4 Jäeger shots!" he turned back to the group and smiled, "this may be a gay bar but it's still the Midwest." And for two hours these three punks bought four shots almost every 20 minutes and always made sure David had two. By 1am David was barely able to stand up. By 1:15, Odin, Rowan, and Cade were cajoling him out the door and back toward his apartment.

"Dijoo you guys wanna come upstairs for a minute?" David had slurred when they got back.

"Oh maybe jusss for a minute..." Odin had slurred back.

And so David led them up the three flights of stairs and into the worst fight of his life.

He unlocked the door and then one of them shoved him in, breaking the key in the lock with the force.

He fell forward into the kitchen and landed on the tile hands first. He laughed a little thinking it had been a drunken accident and then, mid-titter, a boot with red laces made direct contact with his chin.

Once.

Twice.

The third knock was to the ribs and all the air rushed out of David's lungs.

Blinding stars filled his vision as he heard Cade telling Rowan to lock the door and turn on some music.

Rowan tried clicking the bolt but it wouldn't budge so he put the chain on the door and walked to the stereo. He hit play and the room was filled with guitar strings being plucked and then a woman's voice running through a modifier began yelling, "I-I-I-I'm so stupiiiiddd."

Cade started cackling, "Fag music tells it exactly like it is for you homos!"

And then from overhead and behind, David heard the kitchen drawer with the knives in it slide open and the schwink of one of the big knives being slid out.

David felt his lower right back explode in fire and the weight of Cade on top of his legs while Odin's boots and red laces swam in and out of focus.

"Let's get him locked up before the fun really starts. We can make space, if we push the shit out of the way we can really

let loose," Odin was saying as David felt the fire in his back
pulling out.

That was when he realized he'd been stabbed.

He felt as arms grabbed him under the shoulder and dragged
him on his toes into the bathroom before throwing him
akimbo across the toilet and tub.

The lights turned off. The door shut.

Madonna muffled as she sang, "nobody nobody nobody knows
me" and for a moment David passed out and hoped he
wouldn't wake up before the three men in his apartment
finished. David had no interest in being aware of his own
death.

A while later Odin opened the door and rolled David off the
toilet and onto the floor. He opened the lid and then stood as
hard as he could on the spot where Cade had stabbed him. He
stood on his back, full-weight while he emptied his bladder of
all the Jägermeister in his body across the toilet, tub, floor and
David's torso and then turned off the light and left again.

But not before kicking David one more time in the ribs in the
dark and knocking his air loose once more.

As David lay face down in front of the bathroom cabinet
gasping for air his nose smelled something that gave him an
idea. And with that idea came the only thing that could keep
him alive through this, *hope*.

David pulled himself to his knees grabbing the vanity and used
it to get up, almost blacking out from the pain as he used his
right arm to get his knees under himself. He pulled the cabinet
door open and hoped there was enough.

He wasn't *entirely* in the dark, the crack of light under the door was barely a sliver, but it was enough to let him see the ocean blue shine of a bottle of windex under the vanity next to a yellow bottle and a big white bottle of bleach at the back. He didn't know how much time he had, he didn't know why this was happening, or more specifically; *why this was happening to him.* David pulled the Clorox bottle out first, shaking it gently to feel how full it was and then grabbed the spray bottle of Windex and the bottle of ammonia and unscrewed the caps as he stared trying to decide what to mix and when.

He wondered how he had learned this trick in the first place and then remembered.

This was why his mom had sent him to Minnesota to be with his dad. He had tried shooting Frank with the mix after he burned a hole in the carpet and thought if it could melt the floor maybe it could melt Frank.

How had he forgotten about burning Frank's arms with it? How had this been the idea that his brain had flung forward to save him? Because he knew it worked.

It's what Whites in the South had done to pools during Desegregation to run Black people out.

David heard his furniture being pushed to the far end of the room and knew he needed to be ready to act.

There was nowhere to hide in here.

There was no window to get out through or open.

There wasn't even a vent fan.

But how could he do it?

How could he swap places with the three of them?

And then he saw his plan in perfect action and he waited.

He stood in the space the door swung into and lined the
Clorox and Ammonia on the darkened counter, wrapped his
fingers around the trigger of the bottle he'd filled with both in
the space the Windex hadn't filled and practiced holding his
breath.

He didn't think he could get them all in here but he knew he
could get at least one and hope for the best with the other two
after that. And that was when he saw four shoes block out the
sliver of light. He grabbed the handle of the ammonia and
pressed himself against the wall, he looked up and realized the
coming problem. Once they were in, the lights would be
turned on. Frantically, David set both bottles down and began
twisting the bulbs in the vanity loose.
Then the door opened.
In the mirror David saw a hand flick the switch twice and then
the shadows of Rowan and Cade stretch across the darkened
room.
He saw them throw the shower curtain open and that was
when he saw his moment and returned the earlier favor by
bracing himself against the wall and kicking Cade in the kidney
as hard as he could with his right leg. They fell on top of one
another and into the tub in the wedge of light the open door
let in and then he heard boots rushing across the apartment
and the sound of Odin yelling,

"What the fuck happened?!" as he came into the dark
bathroom.

That was when David squeezed the trigger on the bottle and hit Odin directly in the right eye.

Odin spun, swinging wildly and half blind making contact with the door and sending it into the corner of David's forehead.

David hurled the door forward into Odin's own face shoving as hard as he could.

Odin landed on top of the others, and then without hesitating David threw the bottle of bleach and the bottle of ammonia into the tub and pulled the door shut. He heard them screaming, coughing, gagging. He heard them choking and yelling to find the door.

David pulled his bloodied and urine soaked Madonna shirt off and pushed it into the crack at the bottom and pulled on the door with all his might, his back and eyes on fire, as the coughing and banging slowed and then stopped.

He held the door until he heard the final notes of *Die Another Day* turn into the first notes of *Easy Ride* and only let go when he heard the CD click to a stop.

FIRST INTERLUDE

8/1/1921: Portland, Photos, Patriotic Dinners

"*the inspiration*"
~D.W. Griffith, Birth of a Nation

George Baker had won the mayoral race in a landslide. The local klavern members had backed him fully, even if he only knew a few of the men outside of their robes and hoods. He had received a call last night to come to the Multnomah Hotel for a special announcement about the Klan's goals for Portland first and Oregon overall. Mayor Baker entered the lobby and saw King Kleagle, the Exalted Cyclops, and the chief of police. Most remarkable however, was the attendance of Frank Gifford; recently appointed Grand Dragon of the Oregon Klavern chapter. Gifford had taken to the stage to discuss how the Ku Klux Klan of Oregon planned to rid the city and state of all minorities and Catholics and exclusively support Whites Only businesses like Waddles Coffee Shop. The mayor had spoken that evening saying that, "there are some cases of course in which we have to take everything in our hands. Some crimes are not punishable under existing laws, but the criminals should be punished."

While Mayor Baker didn't specify which crimes or criminals he meant the police and attendants clapped and cheered in unison with the Klan members, all with the same level of enthusiasm. All of this was documented and reported by the Portland Telegram along with a half page photo of the local members of the government and KKK standing shoulder to shoulder smiling

for the camera with a headline that read

"CHIEF KLUXERS TELL LAW ENFORCEMENT JUST WHAT MYSTIC ORGANIZATION PROPOSES TO DO IN CITY OF PORTLAND"

the next morning.

Over the next two years more local chapters popped up from Eugene to Salem. In twenty four months most Chinese and Japanese Oregonians had been pushed South to San Francisco or as far north as Bainbridge Island in Washington.

By 1923 Mayor Baker's relationship with Grand Dragon Frank Gifford had become so chummy that cross burnings on Mount Scott and Mount Tabor were commonplace and faced no negative consequence. When Walter Marcus Pierce's campaign moved from Oregon State Senate to the Governor's mansion, the support of the KKK was so overwhelming that it didn't hurt to know Governor Pierce was an openly racist eugenicist who wanted to sterilize all minorities and indoctrinate all children through public education while excluding both Catholic and Jewish citizens. And most of the state went along with it. Either silently so as to not become a target, or, more commonly, because they were Klavern members themselves and enjoyed striking hate and fear into the hearts and minds of their neighbors. Oregon was barely 35 years old and almost every elected official had introduced legislation barring anyone who wasn't White from living there. So one night in 1923 both Mayor Baker and Governor Pierce held a patriotic dinner to honor Frank Gifford for his tireless efforts as Grand Dragon to keep Portland and all of Oregon a *Whitopia*.

Following the Portland Telegram's reporting on the dinner and those in attendance, decent Oregonians demanded recall elections for the mayor.

The first attempt failed entirely. Following the second recall vote, an anonymous robber broke into the elections offices and stole and burned as many ballots as possible. And with that,

George Baker lost his office and faded into near obscurity. The once reviled kissing mayor was relegated to morning coffee at the only diner in town he wouldn't be assailed at, Waddles Coffee Shop. A sign above the door read, "**White Trade Only, Please!**"

Chapter Five

4/21/2007: The Little Owl

*"The Negro women of America must become the teachers of the
White race in this interracial program there will grow up a
strong sisterhood between White and Colored Women
which will be the safest protection
of the ideals for which the NAACP stands."*
~ Beatrice Morrow Cannady, founder, Portland NAACP, 1913

"Molly, you in danger girl."
Oda Mae Brown, *Ghost*, 1990

Rainbow's call late yesterday afternoon with Lisa had gone better than she anticipated due in no small part to Matthew's new position as *"Captain Shithead"* as Lisa referred to him when she heard who he had rented the bar next door to and how *outwardly* racist they had been immediately upon meeting their new neighbor.

Lisa was a lot of things but a bigot wasn't one.

Yes, she had seen an opening in the property game known as Manhattan real estate, but she always came to the buildings when something was wrong. Slumlords didn't do that. Slumlords did things like take bags of cash from racists and look the other way when they called their new neighbors niggers, monkeys, and coons.

By the end of the call Rainbow and Lisa had decided to have lunch the next day in the West Village. They wanted somewhere Matthew would never go and Lisa didn't want the new tenants to know what she looked like in case she needed to visit the bar once it was open.

And that was how for the first time since Woodstock in 1969, Rainbow kept the shade pulled and smoker turned off on a Saturday.

Lisa had given her the address of a restaurant at 90 Bedford Street and told Rainbow to ask for a table at the back if she got there first. Rainbow climbed the stairs out of the Christopher Street Station and made her way around the corner and down the block to the West, then she saw it. The Little Owl.

A red fronted Bistro with a sign that read "open for breakfast" and standing out front was Lisa. It had been over a year since she had seen her but her style was unmistakable.

Lisa, like every other Manhattanite, had fallen victim to dressing as close to a "Sex & the City" character as possible. As she saw Rainbow coming toward her, she raised her perfectly tanned arm and waved, a set of gold bangles jangling as she did.

Rainbow bit her tongue and smiled wide; if there was anyone who could help exorcise these new White Devils from Harlem, it was Lisa.

"It's good to see you looking so well," Rainbow had started, "clearly this divorce was a win for one of you."

Lisa raised her eyebrows and broke into a perfectly white and broad smile. "That's very sweet of you to say Rainbow," Lisa had been afraid this visit was actually an attack. It was why she had suggested The Little Owl in the first place. It was never dead, and midafternoon on a Saturday offered discretion but also at least a couple witnesses if things went south once they got to the meat of the matter. The Hostess sat them in the back without them needing to ask.

"I'm glad you felt comfortable enough to call me," Lisa said, "I'm still not sure I understand correctly what happened."

"No, I think you got it. There's not a lot of confusion when a White blonde woman calls you nigger," Rainbow said flatly before staring daggers at Lisa.

"My God! I thought you were exaggerating!"

"There's not a lot of room to exaggerate when it comes to some racist, new money, bitch calling you a slur."

"No, I know. I guess I'm just confused about how they came to be tenants in the first place."

"Well as far as I could tell, all it took was a duffel bag of money, a handshake, and blaming you for their existence when Matthew sat in my window booth and did nothing while they explained to him they don't eat 'Coon' food."

Lisa ordered a wedge salad. Her appetite was practically nonexistent once Rainbow had described the afternoon before. *How had Matthew been so stupid? How could he not realize that duffel bags of cash were never associated with anything legal?*

Lisa had cleaned him out and left him flat broke.

That was how.

She had realized that the only thing Matthew loved besides money, was Matthew.

So she took away what she could and left him with what her therapist called, "the illusion of money."

"*Nobody* says no to four buildings in Manhattan in a divorce," the therapist had told Lisa in session one day. She had been right.

They owned two sets of four buildings in Harlem. The properties on 116th and a set of mostly empty units on 136th Street.

Her lawyer got Matthew to agree to taking the 116th apartments as a means of guaranteeing income and he accepted without thinking about how that would affect his ability to pay alimony and have rental income for himself.

She had given him the bar with no strings attached. She knew that any potential tenant would have to pass a gauntlet of city approvals and licenses, but most of all, the approval of Rainbow.

The neighborhood on 136th made Matthew too nervous to visit when there was an issue in a unit.

The day they signed the papers he said to her, "Lisa, I don't know how to tell you this, but your lawyer got you a terrible deal. I couldn't even negotiate things into being fair, that's how bad she was."

Lisa swallowed a mouthful of iceberg lettuce and said, "Wait, he told you they were *my* tenants?"

"Yeah. That they own bars all over the country and that he was just the gofer for the keys and the money. But I know what goes on on my block. I know he got those buildings in the divorce. The city sent notices to the neighbors on programs and the inspector told me when he picked up his lunch. Lots of people, White people, *selling*. Lots of notices being mailed out. Moving trucks all over Harlem everyday. Fill a poor Black neighborhood with nice White families and their Internet and Stock Market money and suddenly it's up and coming. Take the money away and now there's no up or coming, just back down to where we were and all the White people going in vans that make them look like pilgrims in search of a freer life in Ohio," Rainbow popped a piece of pork chop in her mouth and chewed.

"I hope you know that's not who I am," Lisa needed Rainbow to know this disgusted her to no end, "do you think it's like, *I don't know*, some sort of racist tavern?"

"I think that's *exactly* what it is. I heard her yelling in German in the backyard about a beer garden while I was checking the meat."

Rainbow looked Lisa over to decide if she really meant to help; or if when the check came she would call Matthew, get some of the cash to keep quiet and ignore it like he was.

"I think about that morning a lot, Rainbow," Lisa could feel her body sending the signal to her eyes that crying was on the way. "I think about John Richards anytime I meet a new tenant or I pass the building."

"Who?" Rainbow asked without making eye contact with Lisa as the check dropped.

"The man who was shot the morning we met and had that first fight."

Rainbow knew who John Richards was, she was just glad Lisa did too.

She decided she could trust her with this.

Rainbow handed three 50s to the waiter and said, "no change."

Chapter Six
6/7/2006: THE VOICE
"Keine schwarzen Leben."
—The Voice

David had either fallen asleep or passed out from the shock but he woke up coughing, holding the bathroom knob and his eyes and back were on fire. He pulled himself to his feet and leaned against the wall as he worked his way to the fire escape window.

It took all his strength to pull the window open and he felt his back start to burn and bleed all over again as he sucked in big gulps of the early morning air.

How could this happen?

He thought of Matthew Shepard.

When David was a kid three men had beaten Matthew mostly to death before hanging him on a fence in Wyoming.

He thought about how *this* is what they must have been giggling about when they met him in the theater after The Omen.

How they had bought him shot after shot and pushed him down the moment they got back to his apartment.

How Cade checked the knife drawer when they first came back and David had changed his clothes.

How annoyed they were when he'd taken them to a gay bar and demanded Jägermeister and filled him with so much of it that he didn't realize he'd been stabbed until the knife was pulled out.

As he sat catching his breath and feeling his back for the wound he realized he had a major problem with no solution in sight.

He had gassed three men to death in his bathroom and he barely knew their first names let alone who they were.

He grabbed the top sheet off his bed and folded it over itself
before wrapping it around his waist and pulling it as tight as he
could to stop the bleeding and be able to move.

David reached into his back pocket for his Slvr and realized
why Odin and Cade had stepped on his back so hard. They'd
been *trying* to break his phone without him realizing and they
had partially succeeded. The screen cracked and lit up funny
but the dial pad worked and even though it was 3:00 AM he
started to call Val. David tossed the phone on the bed without
pressing the green call button.

If he was going to involve someone else in this he had to know
exactly what he was involved in himself.

David stumbled to the kitchen and almost slipped on the pool
of blood Cade had made when he drove the knife in and out of
his back. He caught himself on the counter and opened the
drawer to the right of the knives and rifled through spatulas,
ladles, and tongs before his hand found the handle he was
looking for.

He pulled out the meat mallet Val had bought for him when he
wanted to learn how to make chicken fried steak.

David limped around the wall and back to the bathroom door.
He pushed the door open and it caught on something and
wouldn't budge further.

The fumes hadn't dissipated and he didn't have the strength to
push any harder so he left the door cracked, went back to the
window and fell asleep, head resting on the pane, meat mallet
in his hand as what smelled like someone cleaning cat piss
wafted through the air.

He woke again to the sunlight coming over the buildings across the street and a pigeon cooing on the fire escape. The entire memory of what happened flooded his brain and body as he looked toward the bathroom and saw a spray of blood on the shower wall and immediately and involuntarily threw up all over the floor in front of him.

He crept to the cracked door and could see Cade and Rowan still in the tub and one black leather boot with red laces half in half out on the ledge of the tub.

Odin's body was the first problem. He had managed to turn and get to the door before collapsing. His arm and shoulder were keeping the door from opening further and David wasn't able to muster the strength to push the door any further.

David leaned against the wall and debated whether to dial 911 and get the cops involved or to call Val to see what she would do.

He made it to his bed, crawled in and picked up his phone dialed 9-1- and then deleted them before dialing 773-555-3897.

> The phone rang once, "What happened? Are you okay?"

David exploded into sobs and heaving breaths.

> "I'll be there in 20 minutes. Are you at your apartment?" Val asked as David glanced at the blood on the floor and began sobbing even harder.

By 7:45 Val was downstairs hammering the buzzer to 3B.

By 7:46 she was at his front door and terrified by the broken key in the lock.

"Take a look at me David. David, baby, look at me..."
her voice delicate and doing its best to mask the terror she felt
looking at the blood on the kitchen floor and bed sheet
wrapped around his bare waist like the world's bloodiest obi.
They stood in the doorway staring into one another's eyes
grateful that they were both alive.

As Val peered into David's baby blues, full of tears and panic,
she understood that as bad as what she was seeing was,
whatever she had yet to see would be unimaginably worse.

And yet as David gazed at each of the radiating golden and
honey rays of what he called her "baby browns" his breathing
slowed, his heart rate began to lower.
And the calmer he felt, the more Mama Val's baby browns
filled with tears of their own.

As David closed the door he remembered how Odin had
directed Rowan to lock the door while Cade had pulled exactly
the right drawer open. How he must have been deciding
between the big kitchen knife, the steak knife, and the paring
knife every time he had handed David the next shot of
Jägermeister maybe he had made-up his mind while they had
climbed the stairs back to 3B and straight into Hell singing
Sweet Caroline with every flight. Remembering the
BA-BA-BAs felt like being stabbed all over again. He did his
best to block as much of Val's view of the kitchen as possible.

When he remembered that the bathroom door was cracked open, sunlight washing the blood sprayed wall of the shower, one black Doc Martin with red laces hanging upside down flapping almost imperceptibly as the open window pushed the breeze through the studio and filling it with what smelled like someone bleaching cat piss and pennies; Val was directed by the shoulder to the far side of the bed. She faced the morning, back to whatever they would find in the bathroom when Odin's corpse ceased to operate as a doorstop.

"I closed last night." David could already feel his heart rate racing again as he remembered this entire thing had been his fault. If he hadn't stopped them to ask what they thought of *The Omen* Val wouldn't be here in her house clothes and bonnet before 8:00 AM. He wouldn't be guilty of triple homicide and these three guys would have possibly been found somewhere straight with Jägermeister and Pils and found someone else to pick on and still be alive.

"These three guys came out of *The Omen* and I asked what they thought of the nanny scene...and then we came back here so I could change...and then we went around the corner to the bar and they kept buying me shots of Jager... and then we came back here again..and..and..." David fell apart all over again.

As Val went to hug him she turned her head and saw all the red on the walls and those red fucking laces blowing in the breeze, her brain thought of her favorite song from childhood and she heard her internal monologue singing, "*do your ears hang low do they wobble to and fro?*" Val squeezed David as tightly and gently as she could, digging her nails into her palms and biting her cheek to keep from screaming.

She asked David where his first aid kit was before realizing the likely answer and untied the obi to see what had happened to him so she could gauge how bad what she couldn't see in the bathroom was going to be. There were four vertical marks on his right flank but none were oozing blood and the skin around them was as pale and freckly as the rest of his body.

When they first met, David told her he was from a tribe in Minnesota but runaways didn't have the best reputation for full honesty. But when he still said it a year later she knew whatever he had fled from had to be real and real bad and she never pried again. She thought of him as hers. She had helped so many kids through the years that it was easy to blend a few of them into one person over time, but David was different.
He wasn't rebellious or manipulative.
He was sweet.
He was the definition of a nice young man.

He had fought hard enough to only be wearing a make-shift tourniquet while three boys who, as far as Val could tell, were not small boys, laid dead in his bathroom piled on top of one another like cordwood, their blood splattered like a Jackson Pollock around the room. She knew he was bigger than this moment, no matter what came next. She couldn't help but admire the fight David had when it came down to it and it had come down to it.

"I don't want to upset you," Val began.

"Then don't." David said and winked.

"David, I mean this. How? How are you out here and they're *all* in there? Do you have a gun I don't know about?"

"No. That was nothing short of God."

Val had to bend in a crouch to be able to reach her arm into the crack in the bathroom door and push Odin's body toward the toilet and sink so she could open the door far enough to get in and move him fully out of the way.

It wasn't that she was afraid of one of them suddenly reanimating in the dark, it was still not fully understanding what David had meant when he said he threw bleach and ammonia on them in the dark and then held the door shut until the screaming and gagging had stopped.

How he had thought so quickly about what to do?
Maybe he was right. Maybe it had been God.

As she pushed Odin's body onto its side, face pressed against the vanity cabinet that had saved David's life, the light reflected the wall behind her.
She saw scratch marks in the sheetrock around the light switch and door jamb. An index nail hung loosely from one of the deepest gouges. Blood had trickled and dried to the wall in rivulets below.

Once the door was fully open and Val had twisted a light bulb back into its socket she could see what Clorox and Ammonia did to the skin of White boys and their black T-shirts and jeans.

"So you remembered this in the dark, stab wounds in your back, and you managed to get them all in here at once *and* get out?" Val was laying out how each step in this survival story was more incredible than the last.

"Val it's like I said, God." David hadn't believed in God or Allah or Yahweh or anyone else before last night. Now he felt what happened was bigger than the present moment and the bodies it brought with it.

They managed to empty all of their pockets before needing a break and closing the bathroom door. They found three bill folds, three sets of keys, one Motorola Razr, and two matchbooks with a dog whistle embossed on the outside and an address in Bronzeville written in red pen behind the matches.

"What the hell are three White boys doing with matchbooks for a bar in Bronzeville?" Val couldn't have been more confused if Rowan had an NAACP card in his wallet.

"Do you think this has anything to do with it?" David was holding up a small photo of a black boy whose face was swollen and purple. He didn't look like he was alive. That was when they both noticed the rope around the boy's neck in the photo.

This time Val threw up on the floor.

Val decided they needed to leave the apartment and make sure David was actually okay and not bleeding internally.

David had pointed out that the ER would ask how it happened and Val had pointed out that as far as the staff and the ER were concerned, this was Chicago.
People got stabbed by strangers all the time.

David had avoided serious damage, there had been a few questions about why the wounds looked around 12 hours old, but Val had handled it with the same level of cool she'd had when she'd found David freezing in Hyde Park when he was 14.

"He didn't want to wake me when he came home after the attack. He was wearing his bed sheet tied around himself like a geisha to keep pressure on the wounds when I went into his room to say good morning. Now we're here and he knows knife wounds go right to the ER."

On the way back to David's apartment Val parked outside the ARMY Surplus and told him to lock the doors and wait.
David got out by the time Val took the keys out of the ignition.
Val told him to keep his mouth shut but to be friendly and try not to stare at any missing limbs on the staff or shoppers.

"Hello!" Val beamed at the man behind the counter, "This is my nephew and he is going to Northwestern in the fall and wants to keep his stuff in footlockers and trunks. Do you have any in stock?"

"Oh Hell! We got more footlockers than Gary has feet!" the man behind the counter bellowed with laughter.

"I stepped on an IED and woke up 300 yards away with nothing below my nut sack," Gary smirked at David.

David stared through the glass display case and saw two carbon fiber legs sticking out of camo cargo shorts.

"Thank you for your service and sacrifice," Val said sweetly and earnestly.

"It's okay, girls always said I had two left feet and now I really do! Though buying shoes has become trickier."

Gary walked Val and David toward the back wall and helped Val load three Seward trunks with wheels into the back of her car.

Getting them up to the third floor had been easy enough, they were going up empty.

It was the coming down that was going to be a problem.

"I have to call Vaughn. You're in no shape to carry these back down, let alone load them into the car again. Besides, he has an SUV with tinted windows. He was in gangs when we were younger. Trust me, this isn't his first rodeo."

Vaughn had come, no questions asked.

David laid on the bed with a bag of thawing corn on his back while he heard Vaughn and Val groan as they lifted the bodies and listened to the latches of each trunk click shut.

Val said they would pick up cleaning stuff on their way back from getting rid of the trunks.

She brought David a pain pill and water and told him to clean, chain the door when they left, and rest.

He watched as Val and Vaughn slid all three trunks in the back of the Yukon and pulled the back shut. He saw Val get in the passenger seat and the car drive away.

Then David slept deeply and dreamlessly.

He never saw Val or Vaughn alive again.

When he woke up the Razr he had pulled from Odin's pocket was vibrating and playing a song he had never heard; a man's voice singing *were you born across the water then a member you can't be...*

He decided he would answer but not speak.
A man's voice came through the receiver.
It was deep and steady with the faintest accent, but David couldn't place it.
  "We caught two menschenaffen by the tail..." the voice said.
David could hear two voices screaming out in pain in the background.
One was a man, but he knew the woman's voice the same way he knew his own mother's.
He screamed.
  "Ah... so your mammy's name was Val," the Voice snarled at him.
  "Please don't hurt them! Please don't hurt *her!*" David begged as he heard the phone change hands.
  "Hallo kleiner mann, du hast unseren Odin und Rowan und Cade mitgenommen...das sind drei von unserer Seite, aber wir haben nur zwei von deiner...who bist du, mein Liebe?" a woman asked.
  "Goddamn it Ev, give me the fucking phone back!" the man said, first far away and then into the receiver. "I don't

know who you are, young man, but I can tell you're White from your voice. Be glad we're cleansing the world of these menschenaffen, you deserve to have friends that aren't subhuman." The Voice now hollow and devoid of any emotion.

"Please, I'll do whatever you want. Just please don't hurt *her*. She's the closest thing to a mother I have."

"There's no polite way to say this, but some things just are what they are, and my Vater taught me 'keine schwarzen leben'."

David heard a pistol fire and Val scream.

Then he heard a second shot and the screaming stopped.

The line went dead.

David howled and wailed and sobbed until he felt his back getting wet and realized the stab wounds were bleeding again.

David didn't know what to do.

He'd heard a man say something in German, and a woman *really* say something in German before the Voice yelled at her to shut up and then shot Vaughn and Val before hanging up.

What had he called her?

He couldn't go to Val's house.

What if they found her ID?

He couldn't go to the cops.

At this point he didn't even know where the Voice had found Val in the first place.

Then he realized what she must have done with the trunks.

Where were those matchbooks?

David found one on his bed but not the other and was certain Val had done something stupid that it had gotten her killed.

For two nights David slept where he felt safest when Charlie
had dropped him off so many years ago.
A bench in Hyde Park.
Matchbook in his pocket.

SECOND INTERLUDE

7/14/1921: Very Fine People on Both Sides

"When they go low, we go high."
~First Lady Michelle Obama
on how to handle bullies during the 2016 Election Cycle

"You also had people that were very fine people, on both sides."
~Sitting President Donald J Trump
regarding racially driven vehicular homicide in Charlottesville
during a 'Unite the Right' rally

"Tulsa's Race Riot and the Teachings of Jesus, a Sermon"
by Bishop Edwin D. Mouzon -excerpt

"For the teachings of Jesus are of Supreme Authority. Never man spake like this man concerning God and man's duty to man, Jesus speaks the final word. He is the moral ideal Incarnate. Before his bar we must all stand, not in the last great day only, but now and always. This very day we stand before the judgment bar of Christ, what have we to say about the things which have happened here in Tulsa and which have been written about in every newspaper in the civilized world? It should be known that the relation between White people and colored people in Tulsa has not been different from what one will find in other towns and cities where there are large numbers of colored people the majority of colored people in Tulsa are just like colored people elsewhere— neither better nor worse the majority of White people living here are just as fine people as can be found anywhere in America."

Chapter Seven

7/7/1969: Footsie & Look-see

"One of these days I'm gonna stop my listening,
gonna raise my head up high.
One of these days I'm gonna raise my glistening wings and fly
But that day will have to wait for a while,
Baby, I'm only Society's Child."
~Janis Ian, *"Society's Child"*

It had been four years since the night daddy died. That night those men had forced their way into the dining room downstairs and the apartment door upstairs when daddy told the men there was no money in the till because of what had happened at the Audubon. Nobody went out for dinner after the Minister had been shot. Daddy told them they could take all the meat in the smoker as long as there was no trouble. She'd had just enough time to lock the upstairs door and turn all the lights off before she heard a man yell and then the sounds, muffled by the door, of her daddy being jumped by three laughing voices. Rainbow remembered the sound of someone coming up the stairs, rattling the doorknob and going back the way they had come. That was when Rainbow had tiptoed to the kitchen and struck a long match on the corner of a brick and lit the stove. A cast iron skillet on the back burner, 3 quart saucepan on the front.
Rainbow dropped three bricks of lard in each and prayed for the men to leave her and daddy alone. When she heard the men in the kitchen underneath her, she remembered the door to the back stairs and crept toward it.
Unlike at the front, the door at the back stairs opened out. As Rainbow extended her arm to grab the handle and pull it shut, she looked down the darkened stairway and saw a White man grabbing the cleaver out of the chopping block. As she pulled the door toward her, it groaned and the man looked right up at her. Rainbow pulled as hard as she could, the door slamming shut as she first saw the man turn the handle of the cleaver in his hand and then hurl it up at her like a baseball. She heard the cleaver hit and bounce off the other side of the door before

skittering back down the way it had come. She threw the bolt
across the door but could hear the man coming up toward her,
two stairs at a time. Rainbow felt him pulling on the knob
from the other side with all his might. She waited for him to let
go a little. Just enough to give her space and time to do what
her mind was set on.
And then it came.
    "Come on you little nigra bitch! We don't want to hurt
you, just see if it's true what they say..." the man's voice said
through the door.
    "If what's true?" Rainbow let go of the knob, making
sure the man could tell she had.
    "If you colored cunts have pink pussies!" the man
began to chortle and took *his* hand off the knob.
Rainbow heard him let go, and while she listened to this
monster laugh, she slid the bolt as silently as she could.
When she heard the prickling sound of hair on wood as he
pressed his head to the door to listen, Rainbow flung it open as
hard as she could.
The door smacked into his head and began to reverberate as he
stumbled and then fell backward, somersaulting off the railing
and wall. Rainbow saw the gleam of the edge of the cleaver in
his hand.

She saw him land on the kitchen linoleum below, legs splayed
like a spatchcocked chicken. Right arm jutted out from when
he tried to land in control, left arm bent funny like a chicken
wing under his chest and neck, and then Rainbow saw the
shimmering side of the cleaver facing the ceiling, a band of

silver light appearing from the man's clenched hand and disappearing under his chin.

Then a pool of ruby began to form and rush out across the white floor, dust motes caught in the outer edge of the spreading wave and twinkling in the yellow light.
Another man appeared.
Rainbow pulled the door closed again before he could see her. The bolt slid back into place and she could hear two White men talking in the kitchen about what to do now.

Rainbow remembered the lard on the stove and crept back to the kitchen to make sure the pots didn't overheat. As she turned the flame down on the burners she heard a soft tapping on the door at the front. She knew that rapping-tapping pattern.

Her Daddy's voice came low and weak, "Rainbow are you safe?"
Rainbow threw the door open and saw her bloodied father leaning on the landing, rivers of crimson oozing from his head. She pulled him inside and relocked the door. She helped him down the hall and into bed. She closed the door and turned the key from the outside, sliding it into the vase on the hall table the way he had when she was little and misbehaved and got grounded.

**

Rainbow was remembering that night and daddy and the men while she skimmed clumps of breading out of the oil in the pan on that Monday afternoon in early July when she heard the bell on the door tinkle and then five voices asking one another if they were sure this place was the "real deal."

The Harlem Cultural Festival had started for the third year last night and the neighborhood would be crawling with hippies every weekend through August.

The nice thing about them was their love of good food; Rainbow knew this was probably due to their constantly bloodshot eyes and giggling. But their money was as green as their grass and they loved saying she was a *smoker* too when she brought them brisket by the basket and sat tray after tray on every table in the dining room.

"*How can you know what to look for in a beer?*" a voice on the radio was asking during a commercial break as the sunlight washed the doorway in a bright white aura.

Rainbow dropped a fresh roll of paper towel on the spindle of a four top where a girl with an Afro that rivaled Rainbow's sat playing Footsie with a White boy in a suede vest with green eyes.

"Miss, I'm from Missippi," the boy said, mispronouncing his home state the way all true southerners did, "I got to tell you, y'all make the best damn brisket I've ever had."

"Well, that's mighty kind of you," Rainbow assumed if this boy was willing to play footsie so openly with a colored girl; he must not be that bad and did her best Scarlet O'Hara before walking to the five boys in the doorway. "Hello boys, booth or table?"

The boy in the front of the group blinked at Rainbow and said, "This where that little colored girl cut that man's throat with a meat cleaver and deep fried another one's head?"

Rainbow's heart sank.

Chapter Eight

7/4/2007: Die Blauäugige Ratte

"Wer die Jugend gewinnt, gewinnt die Zukunft."
~Adolf Hitler

"What to the Slave is the Fourth of July?"
~Frederick Douglass

The past two and a half months on 116th Street and Malcolm X Boulevard would have seemed business as usual to anyone unaware of what was happening behind the door of #45.

But inside the bar, behind the yellow and faded newspapers and space for lease banner blocking out the window, four men and one woman were sitting at a metal table on folding chairs. Wagner's *Rienzi* played low while Gunnar spoke.

"Thank you each for your relocation to this sector. As you know, our bar in Chicago burned down last night and the culprit still hasn't been identified or apprehended. We feel we know which hang around it was, but nobody has seen him since yesterday evening."

"Die Blauäugige Ratte," Evangeline said, her red lips opening and closing like guillotines over her perfectly straight teeth.

Gunnar didn't know who she meant, he'd never seen him.

"As you may know, tonight is our true introduction to the neighborhood. Ev has managed to befriend 3 Arya who feel unsafe in the neighborhood and are worried about the number of families leaving the neighborhood this summer alone. They and their husbands have been invited to our party here and have been told to bring any friends who may feel the same way. I ask that you arrive no earlier than 2145 and no later than 2205. This will give you timed alibis so you may each attend the planned boot parties throughout the area. Provided you don't dirty your toes too much, everyone should more or less be able to attest to your presence here and not there. Remember, you represent the *true* America, it should be the junkies and welfare queens who are leaving this city, not the people whose European ancestors settled New Netherland."

Next door outside number 47, Rainbow was bending below the window frame, staple gun in one hand, the corner of a piece of Red, White and Blue bunting in the other.

This was her second biggest day for business besides Memorial Day, and this year's last Monday in May had been slow.
The stock market couldn't make up its mind and since January there had been fewer new White faces moving into the neighborhood and more and more moving trucks pulling away. The economy didn't worry Rainbow.
The first time her mama let her sit at the kitchen table and watch her move all the "greenbacks" back and forth, picking up handfuls of coins and dropping them in perfect little towers, picking up her Black BIC pen and marking something down enthusiastically one minute and then uncapping "The Red Devil" the next, writing something new down and shaking her head, Rainbow had understood that money was a way to keep White Men busy, and Ledgers were a way to keep women aware of what was going on in their homes. She had also worked out that all of it was made-up to keep people like her and Mama and Daddy from ever making it too far up the ladder, lest they pass a White Man along the way toward the top.

She had worked all of that out that first time she watched her mother play the money game, and she was only 11 years old.

When Mama died, Rainbow learned that her daddy could do physical math. 2 teaspoons, half a cup, 6 ounces. But for as good as daddy was at the smoker or cleaning chickens, he couldn't do arithmetic where the outcome didn't end in change and telling the customer to have a blessed day.

She had kept herself afloat throughout Harlem in the 1980s. She had kept the doors open during the gas crisis in the Carter years, and she had managed to keep herself and the barbecue together after those men killed Daddy and she killed them.

Rainbow watched two new honky bastards cross the street and open the bar door. She knew this wasn't an issue with the economy or needing a vacation. This was about the reason she had kept the place after Daddy was killed. It was why he kept it after Mama died and even before that, when Granddaddy bought the lot and built a one room shack out back until eventually made enough to build the house upstairs.
No, this wasn't a matter of Harlem falling into the hands of White people. Harlem had always been big enough for everyone. The problem was that *these* White people had snuck in here, decided this town wasn't big enough for the both of them, and for two months still hadn't taken the sign out of the window, but had managed to call her a nigger the moment they met her and hadn't said a word since.

What were they doing there?

Did she call the FBI and say there was a couple of well dressed racists who paid cash she wasn't supposed to even know about at a bar they went to every day, but never opened the door for even the mailman?

"Would it help you to know they have three young men come every day at 12:00 PM exactly? That one of them wears red laces on his Doc Martens with these huge bows that bounce all over when he walks," she could hear how crazy she sounded. She would turn 63 in August and could tell everyone she was retiring early and move somewhere as far away as she could. She had started drawing her Social Security check last year when everyone said the economy was going to tank. She would have waited until she was 70 to get her full draw but she'd only spent that first check on a birthday trip to Atlantic City to take acid with her friend Judith and see Phish.

They both had August birthdays and Judith had said, "Girl, it's like the summer of love with cuddly White boys and acid, they're half our age! We can be hip old ladies. It'll be fun."

It was fun. Judith called her the morning her check came and told Rainbow to call her back when hers arrived. Rainbow called just after 1:00 and at 2:30 they were giggling with the bank teller about their birthday plans.
They had gone back to Rainbow's and played the money game, first piling the whole stack evenly and then taking out a sheet of loose leaf and two pens. One black, one red. They listed their expenses. Bus fare, hotel food. Concert tickets, T-shirts for souvenirs. They had to guess what they thought the going rate for two tabs of acid and an eighth of weed was, Judith had suggested they ask one of the corner boys and Rainbow stared

flatly back until they both burst into laughter thinking about all of it.

They guessed $20 for the acid, $5 for the weed.

They were officially little old ladies on Social Security.

The last time they bought drugs, they had used their looks to pay. They'd gone to the concert. They bought the T-shirt. But no matter how hard they tried, nobody would sell them acid. They both decided the music was good enough but the pot smoke hurt Judith's lungs, and they went back to the Borgata by 11.

They sat in front of two slot machines, glassy eyed, not betting or moving, just stoned and watching the lights blink until a floor manager came over and asked if they were staying in the hotel and if they needed any help getting to their rooms or medical attention. They had both started laughing so hard that the floor manager began giggling too.

Rainbow held up her Phish shirt and said, "Oooooh," and began laughing again before walking away and telling the waitress they were, "okay, just having a little birthday fun."

The waitress told Rainbow and Judith that she hoped she turned out to be a little old lady like them, while handing each a bottle of water and a bag of Doritos.

Judith and Rainbow hadn't met one racist shithead on that trip. Every person treated them with the same level of enthusiasm as they would have treated their own grammies and nanas.

**

She saw as one of the two men waved at her, that was strange. She raised her hand in return, despite herself. Then she saw he wasn't waving. He was raising his arm at 45 degrees. The Hitler salute. Rainbow realized she was raising her own hand, holding the staple gun. She squeezed the trigger, even knowing how dumb it felt.

Chapter Nine

11/26/1920: Seneca the Younger

"Of the 13,000 Black New Yorkers in 1845,
either 100 or 91 were qualified to vote that year.
Of the voting eligible population, 10 lived in Seneca Village."
-Wikipedia.com (Seneca Village)

The village of *Haarlem* near the northernmost reaches of
Manhattan before the pastures became forest was founded as a
Dutch Colony and named after a village in the Netherlands in
1658. For the first two hundred years it existed as a small
community of almost exclusively German speaking farmers.
In 1857, as was and is inevitable on the Isle Manhattan,
expansion brought development to *Harlem,* and with it
numbered streets, houses, stores, and roadways where
meadows had been only months before.
Most bothersome to the direct descendants of the Dutch
settlers who came in search of undisturbed, simple, peaceful
lives for generations; the now also displaced Negroes from the
former Seneca village pushed north to the farmland when their
homes were turned into a park for White mothers and their
children seeking respite and fresh air away from the bustle and
pollution further down the island.
And for as unhappy as the Dutch were, the Negroes who had
been removed by something called *eminent domain* were no
longer allowed in the park where their own homes had once
stood.

That was how the American Negro had grown Harlem from
meadows to explosions of culture, food, music and style. By
being planted in the same soil as White people who had put off
the inevitable for too long.

On May 26th, 1882 Isaac Jefferson swaddled his first son in the
middle of the night in a tar paper shack by lantern light.

He named him Freeman. Something his son would be for his whole life thanks to President Lincoln, God rest his soul.

**

And now just after midnight on what Freeman's own son would one day call "Black Friday", in a tar paper shack of his own, Freeman remembered his father and mother and how brave they must have been to move here after the city took Seneca and paid his father pennies on the dollar and pointed him and mother North to the pastures. How the White boys had called him *choco* and spit at him when he was little before the wave of southerners had come fleeing Jim Crow.

How most of these boys had grown into hateful young men and moved upstate to Binghamton or out to Indiana, Illinois, or all the way to Oregon in search of their imaginary *Whitopia*.

Freeman had sold father's parcel at the beginning of the year and bought the building out front. It wasn't much, just a wood-slat fronted building with a cellar big enough to work in with a vault light panel laid streetside to get sun in during the day. He'd built the smoker behind that and slept outside most of the summer so he could check the meat during the night.

Business had picked up steadily and by Labor Day he was able to buy the materials to build this shack for the winter and if business kept up he'd be able to build a house on top of the dining room next fall and be able to leave this place to his descendants for at least 100 years.

Freeman looked out the small window toward the smoker and dining room beyond, he could see the edges of the building outlined in black but there were yellow and orange swirls of light dancing against the dark beyond that.

Freeman jammed his bare feet into his Endicott-Johnson boots without lacing them fully; threw his wool coat over his undershirt and ran full speed around the side of the dining room, slowing as he passed the barbecue pit to grab the full pail of water he kept next to the smoker even when it was cold and empty.

As Freeman rounded the corner he saw ghosts. Three men in Klan robes and pointed hoods with black eyes and were across the road watching as a cross burned. Light bouncing off the dining room window, illuminating everything up the colors of Hell.

Freeman tightened his grip of the handle of the pail with his right hand, cupped the bottom edge of the back with his left, and flung the water in a perfect arc at the center of the cross; the mist mixing with the smoke created by the extinguishing of this threat into a billow of rainbow colored fumes in the pale autumn moonlight. And with that, Freeman turned on his left heel and ran full speed back toward the smoker. He heard the men yelling and the sound of falling feet behind him.

Freeman reached the back of the building, braced himself with his left hand on the corner of the dining room and bent down, trusting his memory and body to keep itself alive during the next few moments.

His hand wrapped neatly and instantly around the maple handle of his axe. His left hand let go of the wall and grabbed the handle two thirds of the way up and he put his full faith in God and full weight into spinning in a clockwise half circle, axe swinging full velocity like a sharpened Louisville slugger until he felt the unmistakable connection of the blade slicing into flesh.

He hadn't the money for saws or cleavers when he started, and the axe had set out back since he earned enough for knives downstairs and tools out back by the smoker and now he knew why.

Freeman pulled the axe out of whoever he had hit and heard gurgling before something hit the grass with a thud. He pulled his back against the wall and raised the axe above his head, listening to feet coming in, a voice whispering low.

Freeman saw the pointy white head walk beyond the small alleyway and looked toward the lantern light in the window of the shack. He brought the axe down as hard as he could, crumpling the white cone, then Freeman felt the crunch of skull splitting open travel down the axe handle and up his arms.

Freeman heard the click of a pistol come from the other side of the smoker and a voice with the faintest Dutch accent say, "drop the axe, Choco."

Freeman dropped his hold on the axe and it, and the Klansman it was embedded in, collapsed to the dark ground.

Freeman didn't hesitate, he dropped to the ground and reached forward along the bottom edge of the smoker.

He felt as the edge of the cleaver sliced into the webbing of his right hand, wrapped his fingers around the square blade, and lifted it up and off its hook. He grabbed the wooden handle and turned the cleaver blade sideways and pulled it up to his right shoulder as he crouched in the darkness.

"Come out little Zwarte Piet, I know you're hiding around there, blending into the night. You thought you could come here and put us out of business?"

The man was coming closer, his shoes crunching the charcoal in front of the smoker as he crept, "You people stole Haarlem from us. The city closed Seneca to try and rid New York of your blight, but you coons don't have the brains to understand when you're not wanted."

The man was two steps from the corner of the smoker. Freeman put his weight on the balls of his feet and got ready. The shoes took their final two steps and Freeman saw the man's empty right hand appear first in the shadow of the light in the shack, and then as the Klansman fully appeared, a voice from out front called,

"Freeman? Are you back there?"

The black eyes of the hood tilted quickly up and Freeman didn't hesitate. He brought the cleaver through the night air with a clean *swish* before slicing a straight edge along the gap under the hood that revealed the Klansman's smooth pink neck.

A spray of hot liquid washed across Freeman's forehead. He could feel it in his hair and beating on his scalp as he watched the hooded ghost grab at its throat and fell backward, cracking his head on the paver stone Freeman kept his chair on in the summer.

Freeman Jefferson didn't waste a moment, he knew that the only thing worse than killing three White men was being found with their bodies, covered in their blood.

He pulled the coat off and wiped his forehead with the lining. When he got to his feet he saw his undershirt had a perfect V of red from where the coat hadn't caught the spray. He pulled the shirt off, tucked it and the coat into the smoker and ran back to the front along the other alleyway bare chested in the November air.

Three men and one woman were standing around the smoldering cross holding pots and buckets, looking up and down the street for whoever had done this.

"Did you see anything?" The woman asked Freeman.

"No, I saw the fire and grabbed my pail and came running. I had to go back and get the key to get a bigger pail to fill and then I heard y'all yelling and came back out here, but the fire is out so I thank you for being good neighbors and friends, but I think we can all go back to bed. Free lunch for you all tomorrow."

Freeman thought that all sounded genuine and believable. He just needed them all to agree and not ask to check out back with him.

Everyone bought it and three of them, the men, left without issue. The fourth, the woman, had started to go but then noticed something and lingered.

"Why is your hand bleeding?" She had asked, and Freeman knew there was no way to explain it in a lie.

"If I let you patch me up, can you keep a secret?"

Freeman and Caldonia and Jefferson were married for 27 years and had one son, Charles, born in 1921, in late September.

Chapter Ten

7/3/2008: The Flying Dutchman

"I have every note, every characteristic, motif in my head,
so that when the versification is complete and the scenes arranged,
the opera is practically finished for me; the detailed musical
treatment is just a peaceful meditative after-labor,
the real moment of creation having long preceded it."
~Richard Wagner, Composer

As the lobby of the Metropolitan Opera house filled with a murmurating mass of couples on dates and tourists discovering the magic of Lincoln Center, the atrium filled with voices from every direction saying how they, *"felt like Rienzi was more relevant than ever,"* and the random sarcastic know it all, teenager boy saying, *"did you know it was Hitler's favorite opera?"*

And there, among all the other people, too overdressed to sit in the dark while they silently watched tyranny take hold, David had seen her. The Queen Featherwood herself. Even in the darkened Opera House in 14 rows and 88 seats away, he had seen those Falu lips moving silently along with the ingenue playing Irene.

David scanned the lobby, trying not to stick out in case she had seen him too, or at intermission when the lights had come up.

**

The day he heard her kill Vaughn, and then Val through the phone he had made a plan. He spent six months going from average with baby fat to as close to a believable *hang-around* as he could; in shape but not totally fit yet, and a long way from *Ubermensch*. He had started wearing all black and watching the boys with straight white laces interact with one another and what their tattoos and patches meant. He had learned all his words. 5 words. 14 words. 88 reasons.

He saved two weeks of his paychecks and bought a pair of black steel toed Doc Martens and White laces and learned how to string them through horizontally without crossing.
He had stayed out of the sun to be as White as possible, and on the 8th of January in 2007, he had gone to the address that was written inside the matchbook with a dog whistle on it and prayed he was right.

**

David wound his way down the stairs of the lobby, quickly but calmly doing his best to be invisible, and as he reached the main floor, he saw that blonde Viper of a braid on line at the coat check and accidentally bumped into an older woman from behind.

"Jesus Christ!" the woman yelled, her massive black and gray afro turning as she did, turning David's back to the coat check as she faced him, "do you make it a habit to shoulder check little old ladies at the opera?"

"I, ma'am, I am so sorry. I wasn't watching where I was going. I thought I saw my girlfriend at the coat che–"

"Girlfriend? Baby, it is 2008. Obama is going to be Presi- oh shit, I need you to turn with me so my back is to the coat check."
Her eyes were begging David to oblige, and despite all his instincts, he did.

"Who is it? Old boyfriend? Old *girlfriend*? I mean, *it is 2008...*" David was doing his best to keep her calm while also using her Afro as a way to look for Evangeline without her being able to see him.

"No, it's never mind, but thank you." The woman seemed like it was serious, and given the fact that he knew Evangeline was over there, he wondered if this woman knew her.

"You seem trustworthy," David had been in Manhattan for half a day, but he knew little old ladies are almost never the bad guy, "there's a woman over there I know from back home. I didn't know she moved here. I didn't know she would be here tonight. But right now your hair is hiding me from her. So it's *you* who is saving *me*."

"There is a man, not a boyfriend, a neighbor, a shithead nightmare of a neighbor. So no, it is you who is saving me."

Across the lobby, Evangeline had been digging through her clutch, looking for the chip to give the attendant for their umbrellas and her shawl. But Gunnar had seen *her* come out of the space between the curved staircases, up from the mezzanine and headed toward the bathroom when she saw a *Fresh Cut* shoulder checked her perfectly. So hard, in fact, that the Black bitch had yelled *Jesus Christ* so loud that he heard it all the way over here.

"That Black barbecue bitch is here," Gunnar said to Ev through gritted teeth.

"Who?" Evangeline had found the chip and was handing it to the coat check boy.

"Der schwarze Regenbogen." Gunnar knew how to get Evangeline to focus. He had since they were kids.

Evangeline turned and saw the back of Rainbow's head bobbing as she spoke to someone she couldn't see.

"If seeing her here like a black dandelion has soured the evening for you, go say hello and sour hers," Evangeline turned back to the coat check window and looked for the boy, "you go play, I'm getting our things, visiting the badezimmer, and I'll meet you out by the fountain. *Don't do too much.* Remember we have a surprise for her next month and after what happened in Oklahoma this morning we can't afford anymore fuck ups or fatalities," she handed the coat check boy $2 and a matchbook, handed Gunnar his umbrella and said, "don't use it," and then pointed to the matchbook said to the boy, "we meet on the 8th at 8pm," and walked to the bathroom.

Something tapped twice on the woman's shoulder and a voice from behind her afro said, "*Rainbow*, are you bothering this fine young White man? Son, was this affenfrau ruining your night? I know seeing her bump into you surely ruined mine."
Rainbow watched as this young man's eyes filled with the same terror hers had when she saw Gunnar.

David felt his entire body self-destruct or teleport or disappear into the woman's hair.
What had that voice called her?
Rainbow.
Surely that wasn't really this woman's name.
How did this voice know her?
How did David recognize that voice? Where was it from?

As the woman, Rainbow, turned to face the voice, David saw him, the Ubermensch whose photograph was in every Dog Whistle David had been able to find and burn down in the last two years. *This Voice* had been the last thing Val had heard. *This Voice* must know where Val's body was.

And then *The Voice* introduced itself to David as the Ubermensch held his hand out and said, "Heil, my name is Gunnar and I train young men like you to handle situations like this, *appropriately*. I'd love for you to come by on the 8th at 8," Gunnar handed David a black matchbook with a red dog whistle on it and then said, "Gute Nacht," and *spit* in Rainbow's face in front of the still trickling streams of opera goers before joining them and disappearing through the glass doors and into the warm July night.

Chapter Eleven

7/4/2007: The Sign of the Cross

"Certainly one cannot ban
Cross Burning in the sanctity of his bedroom."
~Antonin Scalia, Supreme Court Justice

"A Cross Burning tells your adversaries that you are coming."
~Barry Black, 1998 interview

As the sun went down on 116th Street that Wednesday evening, Rainbow wondered again who those two men that had shown up were.

How had the one felt so emboldened that he raised his arm in a Nazi salute without thinking twice?
Then remembering she had pulled the trigger on her useless staple gun without thinking reflected that maybe she just knew how to hate him the right way, right away, and that he was an ignorant jackass who had probably never read a history book or grown up with an adult in his life who told him he was wrong.

Rainbow flipped the latch on the smoker and jabbed her thermometer in one of the chickens and watched as the little red arrow climbed across the 80s, 90s, through the low 100s, and then settled in the wedge with a cartoon chicken on it. She pulled the bird and dropped it into a to-go container, nested in a bed of red and white parchment paper and taped it shut.

She closed the door and flung the latch, and then over the wooden fence separating her yard from the beer garden at #45, she saw a large block of wood, it looked like a fence post, *but what was it doing standing on its own in the middle of their yard?*

"Mind your own business, Rainbow," she said to the boxed chicken, "those people are trouble, and the more you get involved, the more trouble you're bound to get into."

In the last two months, Lisa had learned that the Aryan couple
did own bars across America. Almost always in a Minority
parts of town to begin with, but over time, the course of a year
or so, the neighborhoods they were in were completely new
situations.
The people in the apartments around the bars all moved out
and the patrons of the bars that nobody had seen before they
opened, began moving in.

Four buildings in a neighborhood in Texas flipped entirely
from Black and Brown tenants to bald White men that didn't
say hello and never seemed interested in helping figure out who
attacked the latest Black boy coming back from the store alone
late at night.

But that wasn't the worst of it.

Some of these men had been police officers in whatever
podunk place they had lived before and joined the local force
when they moved.

The internet was too much for Rainbow to work out. She'd
had eight-tracks and discmans and BetaMax; they had all come
and gone and at 63, well, almost 63, Rainbow had learned
enough fads for one lifetime.

But Lisa knew what to type in and knew who to call.
She had phoned assessor's offices and licensing bureaus and had
worked out the big picture.

This was a group, a Hate Group.

They hid like a knot of asps in their bars, waiting for someone to disturb their nest so they could strike and release all the venom in their fangs.

The sun set fully around 8:15 and Rainbow pulled the dining room shade.

She flipped the **OPEN** sign to **CLOSED** and pulled the shade on the door. She ended her "closing up ritual" by turning the bolt and climbing the stairs to the apartment.

She grabbed the staple gun off the entryway table and locked the door at the front of the living room.

She turned the switch off to the outside light and walked to the railing of her darkened balcony, staple gun in hand, and watched as people arrived at #45 for the first time that wasn't exactly 12:00 pm.

She saw a mousy woman and plain looking blond man hold up a matchbook to the man working the door.

Everyone who arrived did the same.

Rainbow imagined the conversation going, *"Hi, I'm here for the racist bar. I brought my matches,"* and the man at the door nodding before wordlessly opening it and ushering them into whatever was happening inside.

Around ten o'clock Rainbow saw the glow of a fire coming from the back of the apartment.

She walked through the darkened apartment, past the living room, pausing for a moment as she passed the staircase that the third man had burst in through the night Daddy died, beyond the stove where she had boiled lard in the dark while she begged God to just make the other two men leave once Daddy was upstairs with her. She opened the door to the bedroom her parents had shared, the room where they both died, one from brain *cancer*, one from brain *crushing*.
Rainbow could see the glow of a bonfire through the drawn curtains, but when she eased the shade to the side to look into the beer garden straight on, she saw two horrors, one more evil than the other.

Rainbow looked down at a burning cross and White people, striking matches and throwing them onto the fire yelling, "burn all niggers! Cleanse the world of coons and crack babies!"

And then the second horror, the worst one. Gunnar staring up at her window. She saw him see her, and then he began to smile and wave up at her with one arm at a forty-five degree angle.

THIRD INTERLUDE

7/20/1969: I heard it through the grapevine

"That's one small step for man,"
~Neil Armstrong, 1st man on the Moon, 1 of 12, all Men, all White

On Sunday, July 20th, 1969, the world changed forever. America had done it. They had put a man on the moon in under a decade like President Kennedy had promised before his final car ride through Dallas.
But in the streets of Harlem, on the island of Manhattan, in the City of New York, real history was made as Gladys Knight and Stevie Wonder took the stage at the Harlem Cultural Festival together, singing *I Heard It Through the Grapevine* while a crowd of thousands sang the chorus before breaking into a chant of "We could have spent the money on Earth!" all captured by CBS News cameras, but never released and sits in a vault to this day.

History would forget "Black Woodstock" for almost half a century, only reflecting when archival footage from other sources began being compiled into a documentary by Ahmir K. Thompson in 2021.

Chapter Twelve

8/4/1944: Anne, Judith, Rainbow

*"I must uphold my ideals, for perhaps the time will come
when I shall be able to carry them out."*
~Anne Frank, Diary of a Young Girl

Friday, August Four, Nineteen Hundred and Forty-Four was a warm and sunny day in both New and Old Amsterdam.

On 116th Street in Harlem, Charles Jefferson had finished loading the smoker while his wife, Caryn, had gone into labor. He had run to the bar next door to ask Bill Monroe, owner of the Black and Tan, to mind the meat while he took Caryn up to Harlem Hospital so he could meet his baby.

That had been just before eleven in the morning.

Chuck wasn't allowed in the room, and Caryn told him they needed the Friday money now more than ever, but that he could come after close to hold the baby and name him.

Chuck was convinced it would be a boy. His father, grandfather, and as far back beyond that as anyone knew had been boys. It was a lot of responsibility naming a baby, it would be who they became through the course of their life. He thought about his daddy, Freeman Jefferson. He thought about his granddaddy, Isaac Jefferson. All these men were given names of great stature and importance, and now Charles "Chuck" Jefferson would have to do the same. Name a name and teach it its place in the world.

At just after 10:30 in Old Amsterdam, a little girl woke up for the 761st day behind a bookcase hiding a room that she and her family had hidden inside of since a little over two years ago.

As Caryn filled out paperwork; half a world away, a little girl
named Anne was frantically writing in her diary for the final
time.

*As I have told you many times, I am split in two. One side
contains my exuberant cheerfulness, my flippancy, my joy in life
and, above all, my ability to appreciate the lighter side of things.
By that I mean not finding anything wrong with flirtations, a
kiss, an embrace, an off color joke. This side of me is usually lying
in wait to ambush the other one, which is much purer, deeper,
finer.*

Caryn's labor moved along quickly, and as a light rain fell on
the roof of the Women's Ward of Harlem Hospital, the sky,
wan and gray for a moment, what had started just before eleven
a.m. was over. The church bell rang out six times as Caryn's
baby let out its first wail and the doctor laid the baby on her
chest and stepped away, congratulating Caryn for remaining so
calm during the worst of it and ended by saying, "this little girl
was born in a sunshower, may her life always be filled with
rainbows."
At quarter past seven that night, Chuck came in holding a
bouquet of carnations.

"I couldn't decide on a color, so I told the man to give
me a rainbow," he walked toward the bed, set the flowers
down, kissed Caryn on the forehead, and asked, "now, where is
my Son?"

"Well, why don't you tell me his name first?" Chuck saw the corners of Caryn's mouth curl up at the edges like the cat who ate the canary.

"Now, I've been doing a lot of deep thinking on this, Caryn. I know a name is all a man has to build his life on, Jude. Like from the New Testament, he exposed the false prophets and gave his people the strength to have faith in the stand up for what's right and decent. And you know why my daddy was named Freeman, I want our son to do great things and defeat great evils." Chuck looked at Caryn, she looked ready to cry.

"All of those things will happen, Charles. The world will know our *daughter* for the righteous warrior she is." Caryn scanned his face to see if he had heard her.

Charles walked wordlessly to the bassinet and looked down. A chubby cheeked baby girl with his eyes stared back at him and cooed.

"Judith. Like the Old Testament sent by God and given great intelligence to destroy King Nebuchadnezzar's Army and slay Holofernes."

Charles saw a woman his mother's age in his daughter's eyes. He saw her running the barbecue and not letting anyone be cross, crass, or disrespectful.

"I was thinking *Rainbow*," Caryn said, "like how God gave Noah the rainbow and dove to let him know the flood was over."

Charles stared into the golden and caramel orbs of his daughter's eyes and said, "We'll name you Judith Jefferson and call you Rainbow for short."

That was how Judith had never been called by her real name, except by her best friend, her whole life. It was why those hippies who came to Black Woodstock to escape their White peers upstate in August of 1969 had come up with the name of the baby girls they gave birth to in May of 1970.

All while Gladys Knight sang as Neil Armstrong took one small step for man.

People met Judith Jefferson her whole life and only ever saw the Rainbow, never considering the storm inside.

Chapter Thirteen

9/8/2008: Brenda, Garfield, and the 14th 8th at 8

"I don't like Mondays."
~Garfield the cat

"I don't like Mondays."
~The Boomtown Rats

"I don't like Mondays."
~Brenda Spencer

Rainbow opened her eyes that Monday, thought about that little White girl from the 70s who shot those kids going into the school across the street from her bedroom window and used her daddy's rifle to do it as they said goodbye to their mommies and walked toward the front door before collapsing dead on the sidewalk as the echoing boom of gunfire rang out and adults screamed at kids to get down.

She thought about Garfield and how much he loved lasagna, but not Mondays. She imagined that girl and the cartoon cat and that song by that band with the terrible name and sat up, feet swinging off the side of the bed.

Rainbow looked up through the window at an overcast sky, pressed her hands into the mattress and rose to her full height, back and hips cracking and popping along the way.
She stepped to the window, her gaze tracking from the gray sky to the tarred roof of #45 next door and the beer garden behind that.

And for the 14th time, Judith knew today was the 8th.
At 8:00 PM her window would glow and flicker.

Judith knew that if she opened the curtain even a crack, she would see him down there tonight, looking up at her bedroom and smiling while the colors of Hell illuminated his face and perfectly raised arm.

The rest of them had started wearing hoods and robes, but Gunnar never covered his face. He wanted those people *and* Rainbow to see him in his orange robe with an enormous GD and dragon embroidered on it.

He wanted them all to know, Rainbow especially, that *he* was in charge. They could all be intimidating, but Gunnar knew how to dig it, what really scared people.

She pulled the curtain shut and went into the bathroom to get ready for whatever fresh hell the day would bring.

When the mail came at 1:00, Judith took a pile of red envelopes from the mailman without looking up. The White Economy was nervous Barack Hussein Obama would soon hold the keys to the Kingdom and set the zoo free.

She had meant to sell the place and move out West to Palm Springs at the beginning of all of this. She had felt too old to still be fighting White people about made-up hierarchies and fabricated non-truths.

She was too old to still be having dipshits coming in every few years asking if she knew what happened to the little girl that slit those Klansmen's throats and fried them up for customers.

Rainbow hadn't slit their throats and fried them up. The one man had slit his own throat when she had caught him with the back staircase door. The second man had come up the same way as the first. He had pulled the door open, snapping the bolt and sending it pinging into the darkness as his hulking shadow blocked out the light creeping up the stairs behind him. She remembered grabbing a towel and wrapping it around the handle of the saucepan, lard popping and bubbling inside. She remembered seeing his hand fumble against the wall in the dark, searching for the switch.

She remembered how *Rainbow* had thought to boil the lard, but how *Judith* had remembered the towel so she wouldn't burn her hand.

She squatted down like a baseball catcher, handle and pot ready to swing up into this man's face. He had found the switch and as he did, the apartment flooded with light. The man squinted, but *Judith* had remembered to close her eyes until she felt light on her lids, and that half second had made all the difference. The lard flew, sizzling against the air in a clear stream, and landed perfectly on the man's face.

He began to scream but his mouth filled with liquid hot lard and came back out carrying blood and bubbling pieces of skin. He had clawed at his eyes as his lids fried and shriveled, his right eye whistling like a tea kettle before bursting like a boil. His body writhing and banging on the wall, his elbow smashing the switch, sending Judith back into darkness as he fell to the floor and twitched to his death.

And the third man?

The police never found him and over time, the people who thought they knew the story only remembered their being two; the cleaver and the lard.

Sometimes Rainbow wondered if the third had been real, or if other people knew better what happened to her than she did herself.

But then she would remember.
She could see him clear as day, his EJ boot appearing in a flash of light from the front staircase. The explosion of dust and wood splinters, hanging for a moment, glistening and then bursting into curlicues of debris before the boot became a knee, became a leg, became a body. Giant and clearly muscular even in the dark, his forearms the size of the big can of Peaches at the grocery market.

**

Rainbow moved, but Judith was still catching her breath, because she set the saucepan down, and then wrapped both hands around the handle of the cast iron skillet and felt her palms erupt like volcanoes as they sent white hot electric signals to her brain that the pan was too hot and that she had forgotten the towel when she changed weapons.

Rainbow tried to turn and throw the boiling lard even as she felt her fingertips fry against the semi rough edges of the pan. But the physical shock was too much and instead of throwing the lard toward the Goliath's shadow, she threw it onto the floor in front of her as the skillet tipped to the right, creating a downpour of hot fat that splashed against the pine board floor and sprayed outward in every direction like a molten lawn sprinkler. Rainbow felt beads and waves of fire hit her bare shins and ankles, soaking into her Ked-Peds and burning her toes.

She fell to the floor, grabbing her legs and yelling "Jesus Christ" as she did. She saw the Goliath move toward her in the dark. She watched as the steel toe of his boot connected with her forehead right between the eyes.

Judith heard the Goliath say, "Sounds like you got a taste of your own medicine, dumb nigra bitch," and then watched the boot arc a second time through the shadows and felt it hit her right temple, knocking her unconscious and plummeting her into a dreamless abyss.

**

Rainbow woke up and looked around.
It was the middle of the afternoon.
A poster that read "HOPE" sat in both lower corners of the window.

She looked down at her hands.
They were 64 years old.
She looked at her shins.
They were also 64.
Her hands weren't burnt any more than they usually were.

Her shins had healed with time, the outer side of her right shin gleamed, smooth and hairless.

You'd never know it was a scar unless you knew *why* it was a scar instead of a photo of an autopsy report.

Rainbow was here in 2008, 64 years old, with the KKK next door and a 14th Cross ready to burn just for her tonight at 2000 hours like they had been on the 8th of every month since last July.

This wasn't a dream or a memory.
This was a living nightmare.

Out on the street and around the neighborhood, there were folding tables and stands selling hats and pins and stickers and mugs and anything else that could endorse a Black Boy to the White House.
But not on 116th Street.
Not while those Klansmen met in secret once a month.

All the other soul food, fried chicken, chopped cheese and barbecue joints had been raking in the tourist dollars hand over fist. But not here.
Not at Rainbow's Joint.

Here it was all final notices and bad memories that felt too much like insufferable currents.
The wall phone rang.

"Rainbow's Joint. This is Judith," she said.

"Rainbow, did you say *Judith*?" Lisa's voice asked.

KAPITEL VIERZEHN
8/8/08

"Yet what we suffer now is nothing compared to the glory he will reveal to us later."
~Romans 8:18

"20,20,24 hours to go. I wanna be sedated."
~The Ramones

At 6:00 AM on Friday, August 8th, 2008, Gunnar Erichsen rose out of bed and went to the kitchen of the apartment he and Evangeline had moved into a week before on 136th Street. He opened the door to the refrigerator and the bottles of Pilsner lining the bottom shelf rattled. He reached into the cold white light without looking down and pulled one of seven containers of a dozen eggs out and swung the door shut with his elbow. The bottles jangling back into icy darkness, he pulled an empty beer pitcher from the dish rack next to the sink, blew an adventurous but off course cockroach out of the bottom and began cracking all 12 eggs into the vessel. He needed his morning protein almost as much as he needed his 0540 to 0600 sleep.

He had used his nach stunden to assemble the bunks that arrived yesterday afternoon.

Everything had to be perfect today.

It was their day.

Once every 100 years did this date occur.

8/8/8. HEIL. HEIL. HEIL.

Gunnar turned on the news and dumped the eggs into his open mouth.

"Democratic hopeful, Barack Hussein Obama is expected to speak later this weekend—" Gunnar jammed his enormous finger into the power button and threw the pitcher into the sink so hard that it almost bounced out. Then, still furious, yanked the cord for the TV out of the socket, the force pulling the small set off the counter. It landed on the tile floor and shattered open, plastic ricocheting off the lower cabinets.

Gunnar roared with anger. It was just after 6:00 AM and that Great African Ape with a fake birth certificate had already thrown shit on his momentous day. Evangeline heard the tinkling of egg shells on the edge of the pitcher and the plunks that became burbles as the full dozen went into the bottom. She had listened as the TV had started, heard Gunnar throw a fit, and decided that if this was how today was starting; She would need to get a handle on it fast so it didn't spill through the day and into tonight. They had spent the last month coordinating and relocating everyone from Oklahoma to hotels and campgrounds around Binghamton and through the Poconos and on the couches and air mattresses of members of other chapters of the Brotherhood. They had used the money from the insurance claim on the bars in Austin and Tulsa to pay for those 30 units on 136th Street and a connection they had at a children's furniture store to buy 175 twin bunk beds. At least six in every unit. The ability to put four triads in each apartment and let the red laces from every group of three figure out whose leader deserved top bunk.

Evangeline walked into the kitchen fully nude. She looked at the flat screen on the floor at Gunnar's feet, and lowering herself onto her knees next to it, looked up into his glacial eyes and said, "Las mich die Wut aus dir saugen, Bruder."

Gunnar looked down at Evangeline and said, "Kein Samen soll heute vor Negerblut vergossen werden, Schwester."

And then, from the bedroom, a phone, then two phones, began playing the first notes of Horst-Wessel-Lied.

Both phones ringing out that song could mean only one thing.

Mutter was calling one of them, and Vater was calling the other.

Gunnar and Evangeline Erichsen ran toward their calling parents the same way they had as Kinder when it was too close to supper for them to be playing in the woods.

"Mutter! Vater! Was ist es?" The Erichsens could hear their parents screaming and fire burning in the background.

Then at once, both lines went dead.

At 10:15 AM, David got into a taxi cab at LaGuardia Airport. At 10:35 AM, the cab turned right on 116th Street and stopped next to the curb on 5th Avenue.

"Son, don't take this the wrong way, but I don't know that you realize what partta town this is." The cabbie looked at David in the rear view and saw him popping brown contact lenses into his hand.

"Mister, I don't think you know what part of town this is either, so mind your own. Before I mind it for you." David had practiced being a shithead so much that he didn't sound anything but genuine when he said ignorant shit anymore. He got out of the cab, handed the driver a slightly burned $50 bill, and then seeing his doubt about the usefulness of the cash, pulled two clean 20s out of his wallet and flicked them onto the empty passenger seat and said, "don't pick up anyone who looks like me tonight," and walked toward Lenox.

David reached the northeast corner of 116th Street and Malcolm X Boulevard and turned right. He walked past the grocery store that ate up most of the space on this block and looked exactly like it must have when it opened around the year he was born. He had gone in only once very early into his nesting phase, before he'd accidentally finally met that vile Voice and put a face, handshake, salute, and matchbook with the name last month along with leering the heads of little old ladies and their prunes of husbands bobble faces caked with disgust and disbelief as a perfect egg of loogie, snot yolk and all, emerged from underneath a mustache that would have made Nietzsche question his manhood, fly through the air and land in a 60-something-year-old Black Woman's face.
The sound of the "Gute Nacht" blending with him clearing his throat and hitting David's ear at the same time the woman, Rainbow, received the part that was directed at her.

**

David had handed her his pocket square and said, "mine would have been worse. So again, you saved me," before going into the family bathroom, locking the door, turning the light off and sitting by the toilet on the floor, never taking his eyes off the bar of light in the gap at the bottom. He watched as a slow moving shuffle of feet went in and a sporadic burst of two, four or six feet would come out.

He held his breath as a big set of feet and two smaller feet next to them knocked. One voice asking if anyone was in there; the other voice demanding that she was "going to ruin my dress with pee again" if the door didn't open before bursting into little girl sobs and the big feet, saying "not again, *please*, not again," before hurrying into the men's room, new voices yelling and feet running toward the doors and exits.

David had waited and waited. He could wait all day. He had gotten great at waiting after that *Featherwood* killed Val while that Voice, that face, that Ubermensch watched and spit drivel that hadn't changed in 400 years. David could wait for Hell to freeze over. The problem with this waiting was twofold. First, the Voice. The immediate flood of pain. The urge to say fuck it and finish everything he could with a penknife right there in the lobby of the Met while Rainbow saw what it looked like if he *did* bump into someone intentionally. But what he thought was some weird local gang had turned out to be a nationwide open secret if you knew who to ask and how to listen. They called it "dog whistling" as an honorific to the Schäferhund who tended the flocks on the farms in the good days, and watched the fences for Jüden when the Führer led the entire German flock toward a final solution to the problems of the Aryan people.
But secondly, hearing Gunnar speak and finally knowing what his enemy's eyes looked like; and then being trapped in a bathroom the way he had the night he had fought for his life and won, only to lose the only thing more precious to him than his own life because of it made David's heart quicken. He

began to hyperventilate, and as he pressed against the toilet, he passed out.

Rainbow had wiped the mucus and saliva off her face in one swell foop and folded the kerchief before wrapping it in a couple of the Kleenex from her purse and zipping it inside her coin pouch. She had gone back down the walkway to the mezzanine, saw an usher turning people away, and then she pulled out one of her earrings and dropped it under the other Kleenex in her purse.

"Excuse me, I-I got up to applaud at the end, and I think I clapped so hard I knocked my earring out." Rainbow grabbed the remaining earring by the bottom of the edge and jiggled it gently.

"Ma'am, I'm sorry, but the Lost and Found opens at 10:00 tomor-. Sorry. Saturday, because of the holiday." This usher took security seriously.

"I understand, but my grandson bought me these and he's in the bathroom. If he sees I lost one, he'll be devastated. He's a homosexual. You know how much earrings mean to them." *What the hell was she saying?*

"I'm sorry for that, ma'am, but policy is policy. I'm for the other guy, but I got a queer cousin. I know how it is."

Rainbow swung for the fences. "Me too, for the other guy I mean. My grandson is visiting from San Francisco. You know how people get about Black Conservatism, especially with this guy running," Rainbow pointed at her Obama earring.

"Look, now that I know that, what kind of traditional values would I have if I didn't let a little old lady look for her earring?" The usher let her go look.

After 25 minutes, the usher told her the lights were on timers and would be shutting off soon. Then he asked where her grandson was.
She bent under a seat she had pretended to check four times and pulled the earring out of her purse and held it up.
The usher walked her into the empty lobby and then to the men's room to find her imaginary grandson.

David saw four feet, a man and a woman, walk across the brick of light.
He pulled out his penknife and crouched.
He heard a different voice that he recognized from the men's room.
"Jamal? Jamaaaal? Are you in there, baby?"
David didn't hear Jamal respond. *Had Gunnar and Evangeline done something?*
The man's feet appeared in the gap. "Hello? Hello?" a voice David had never heard.

He got up, flushed the toilet, ran the sink, turned on the light and opened the door.
Rainbow.
David had no clue what was happening.

**

David snapped out of his daydream memory that he had slipped into on the two stops he'd ridden on the 2 train back down from 125th. He had decided to snake his way home. He couldn't believe he made it through TSA in Florida at seven this morning, smelling like fire leaving Orlando.

David came up the back exit of the 110th street stop, turned around the chicken stand that divided Lenox and Adam Clayton Powell Boulevard and walked under the scaffolding attached to the facades of apartment buildings that had been under renovation before the economy went bust. Grateful for the cover, the mesh fencing stapled to the street side, hiding anything behind it from passing cars.

When Gunnar handed him the matchbook at the Met he had felt like he'd found a golden ticket to the worst version of a Wonka factory. When Gunnar had spit in Rainbow's face he had decided not to go to the July meeting, afraid someone in Tulsa would have flown out and recognized him.

Instead he had flown to Orlando on the 7th of last month to lay down a plan to cut one more head off the Hydra. It had been too easy. The little old couple who ran the Orlando chapter had both doted on him the entire meeting on the 8th of July. At the end of the meeting, as a cross burned in the beer garden of the Orlando Dog Whistle, it had been David who suggested they take a photo.

And there, in the amber and orange light, three people in Klan robes, 2 white and one orange, stood against the Falu wall. Under his hood, David smiled a real smile. A satisfied smile of a man who had a plan to take from his nemesis what had been taken from him.

Evangeline's Mutter and Vater.

Finding Gunnar had been next to impossible, his parents a mystery. He himself only finally identified definitely last month as the loogie flew. But David knew that with three of the Whistles blown and burned down, their local leaders locked inside, choked to death on smoke and fumes, he was close to the end. By the end of the year, this would all be over.

"Hey there, go, my friend!" a woman's voice yelled from a doorway.

David recognized it and called back. "Didi, there's my friend."

"I saw some men coming and going all morning. *Or somethin' like that.*"

Didi was sweet, a mentally ill woman who sat on the curb all day drinking dollar bodega beers and watching everything while everyone ignored her.

"Coming and going from where?" David handed Didi five dollars.

"Down by Rainbow's. *Or somethin' like that.* Carrying in big boxes of white sheets. *Or somethin' like that.*"

Didi must be nervous to be this drunk before noon.

"Bed sheets," David said, knowing they were fresh robes and hoods. "Did they have anything else?"

Her face went crooked. Her eyes looked up and down the empty sidewalk. She put the money in her shoe and looked

David square in the eye and said, "big old wooden table and red and white tablecloths. Big plastic thing filled with hoes and spades and trowels and sickles." Didi's eyes wandered to a different thought as she said, "So I came over here where they couldn't whoop down the block at me. *Or somethin' like that.*"
David knew what the men whooping at her meant.
He pulled the side pocket of his backpack open.
He pulled out two blackened $100 bills.

"Didi, I know I just moved here, but you and I are friends, okay? I worry about you. I need you to listen to me and do what I tell you. okay? Take this and go. Go to Queens and get a hotel for a few nights. Go to the Port Authority and buy a ticket to DC. Go to a friend's place and lock yourself in and go on a bender all weekend. I don't care what it is or where you go, but you cannot be out here this weekend. It isn't safe, okay?"

Didi took the money, realized how much it was, looked to David and knew he meant it, and said, "Or. Somethin'. Like. That."
David hoped she meant it.
He hoped he didn't see her for at least a week.
He checked his watch.
11:11, make a wish.
David had less than 40 minutes to change, shower the smell of fire out of his hair and either hole up til dark or get out of the neighborhood for as long as possible before 20:00 hours. He rounded the corner on 116th and saw down the block, a Black dandelion putting out a sandwich board.

Rainbow stood outside the restaurant, hands on her hips,
looking at the sign she had pulled out of the back corner of the
basement this morning, along with the banner she had made in
the Summer of Love. **BRISKET BY THE BASKET**, one side
of the board said, the other read **8 RIBS $4**. The **$4** had
recently been taped over with a napkin that said **$8**.
Rainbow had grown to hate this sign that summer in 1969.
At first it brought in business by the busload.
Then people, *White People* started telling everyone that the
sign offered such a good deal because of what happened to her
and Daddy, and that the ribs were human meat.

As Rainbow looked up from the sign, and then West toward
Morningside Park, so she didn't have to see #45 any more than
she had to today; Rainbow saw a ghost, her grandson she'd
only met once when she had lied about him, even existing.
Jamal waved at her from outside #53, but he was headed her
way and looked worried.

"What the fuck are you doing here?" David wasn't
afraid like Rainbow thought. He was pissed. He grabbed the
sandwich board with one hand, the two sides sending a clap
both ways down the block.
He took two big strides and was inside the dining room, staring
at Rainbow, frozen and confused, still on the sidewalk through
the dining room window.
Rainbow realized she was outside without her staple gun, and
matched David's enormous strides until she too was in the
doorway with him.

David closed the door, locked the dead bolt, and disappeared into the kitchen in the back. Rainbow paused and remembered the last time she and a White Man had been in this kitchen, how they'd been even further down in the cellar, but that only one of them had come back up. How the cops had received reports of three White Men but only found two dead ones and Daddy. How she had put him out of her mind for almost half a century. Rainbow felt something inside her begin to crack. Then David came around the corner and *Judith* realized she may be breaking apart completely.

"I thought you said he was your neighbor. The night we met." David was reeling at this development. *How could he have not seen her a single time before now?*

"We are," Rainbow said.

"And work next to one another, too? You hate one another. That, or you have the most inappropriate relationship I've ever seen. Do you take the bus together too? You in the back? Him and that Sigyn wannabe in the front?"

Rainbow heard the word 'front' come out of David's mouth at the same moment she felt her hand sock his ruddy lips.

"Jesus Christ!" This time it was David's turn to yell it out.

"You think because you see one Ubermensch hawk a loogie in my face that I let any peckerwood say whatever they want to me without getting their cracker ass cracked?"

"No ma'am, I apologize. I, I've had a very long night. I have almost no time to get myself together and out of here until tonight." David checked the wall clock, a black and white cat with eyes and a tail that swung, ticking and clicking as he watched the second hand lapping the hour and minute hands, 11:18.

Rainbow watched him trail off as he stared at the Kit Kat clock looking around the room.

Judith considered something and then Rainbow said, "Don't tell me you're one of those social justice warriors. That clock was my mama's and has never needed new batteries. Don't tell me about it. Bad as those people who come in asking if it's true," Rainbow tried not to wince.

"If what's true," David raised his eyebrow.

"If the KKK is open for business next door."

"Oh." David pretended not to know. "The guy from that night?"

"Yeah, the guy from that night," Rainbow remembered that night and that other night.

"I-I, I was up here seeing where the meeting was." David heard himself and said, "I was disgusted by what he did. I was only in town that night through Sunday morning looking at apartments. But now I was going to go and then tell the cops if it is what I think it is. But I wanted to check it out in the daylight. You know how dangerous Harlem can be."

"I've lived here, right here," Rainbow pointed up to the ceiling, "since the second day I was alive. That man, the KKK, God Herself, won't take this from me. The only time I remember my neighborhood being dangerous at night started April of last year and every night since. And one night in 1965 when Malcolm X died in front of me and I ran home to my Daddy in tears, Ked-Peds icy and wet, totally out of breath." Her gaze leveled itself at David.

"Honestly, I don't know him. I didn't know you worked and lived here, and I am planning on going to the NYPD if he is part of the KKK," David lied, cool and placidly.

"I'll believe you," Rainbow said, "you are my grandson after all," remembering David's face as he had told the usher at the Met his name was Jamal with that same blank face. Almost daring her now, and the usher then, to call him a liar.

"I have to leave now." David watched the cat click its way to 11:21.

"What did you call her?" Rainbow caught herself.

David realized what he'd done, all the cool leaving his body, his face flushing Crimson. Rainbow put her hand on the butcher block.

"Sigyn, Loki's wife. They're very into Norse mythology," David saw Rainbow's hand edging toward the cleaver. "I really don't know him. I know her. I know her. She was who you saved me from. I know her from Chicago. From their bar there."

Rainbow looked at David and stopped moving her hand. "Their bar in Chicago burned down a year ago. I heard her yelling into her phone in the backyard for a week."

David looked at Rainbow, then the clock, then the door. "I have to go, but I'll come back tomorrow, around noon," He was testing her observation skills.

"Come at 10:30. They get here at 11:15. Most days. Three guys come exactly at noon, except on the 8th and 9th.

On the 8th, all five of them come at 8 along with more and more strangers. But today, only he and the three others did, and on the 9th, they don't come at all."

Rainbow thought about showing him the notebook she had filled for the first six months they'd been here. How the cops had said it wasn't a bar, that, even if they'd burned crosses, it was free speech. It was almost 50 years after the murder of James Powell, and the NYPD was as crooked and lazy as ever.

"Oh." David's talking had done almost enough damage. He'd had no sleep, flown twice since sunset yesterday, had to figure out what he'd do if he saw Evangeline tonight and had killed two old people this morning on top of everything else, he walked to the door.
"10:30 tomorrow in case they come at 12. Oh wait, tomorrow's the 9th. Come whenever."
"I'll be here at 10:30 just in case tomorrow is different." David unlocked the door and went left toward where he had come from. Rainbow walked to the door, propped it open, and picked up the sandwich board. She stepped onto the sidewalk just in time to see the door to #45 open. Gunnar stepping outside, Bluetooth set blinking in his ear, gesticulating wildly. Rainbow made herself big in case David was still walking up the block behind her, Gunnar turned toward her.
She clapped the sign open, **8 ribs for $8** facing him.
A smile crept across his face.

Rainbow thought about those teeth glowing in the firelight of the burning crosses she had seen turn to embers, smoking and charred grass on the 8th of almost every month since last Independence Day.

She saw his teeth even and straight and remembered the brisket in the smoker.

She turned toward the door.

She saw Gunnar raise his arm and then spit on the ground toward her.

She remembered she didn't have her staple gun and half ran inside.

At 11:28, Gunnar's phone played the first notes of Ride of the Valkyries.

His heart filled with dread.

"Mein Wido was ist los?" He hoped keeping things in the tongue their Mutter had taught them would keep him and her *ruhig*.

A voice shrilled into his ear, "They were burned alive, tied to crosses in the Biergarten!!" She howled with agony, heaving sobs punching Gunnar's ear.

He unlocked the bar door and went onto the sidewalk for some privacy, "Unsere Eltern werden nicht umsonst gestorben sein. Wir werden diese Blauäugige Ratte finden und sie vergaßen, so wie der Führer zuvor so viele Ratten vergast hat."

"He put their hoods on them backwards so they died in *Schwärze*, Gunnar! He knew them well enough to be here alone with them at 06:00 today."

"OK, we'll enhance security tonight here. The Portland meeting is leadership only. Come home. Stay home tonight and play with Pistenraupe."

"I'm already on my way to the airport. I'm going to Portland. I land there at 19:05. They want a report."
Evangeline hung up.
Gunnar saw that Schwarzer Löwensahn, two 8s on her sign, and knew she was taunting him.
He raised his arm and spit, as dumb as it felt.

Gunnar walked back into #45 and saw the picnic table in the Biergarten disappear under a wave of red and white gingham.
Gunnar pulled a whistle out of his pocket and blew.
The two White Laces clipped the corners of the tablecloth down without looking toward him as he stared at the backs of their heads bobbing in the pre-afternoon combination of cool shade and white hot sun rays.
They didn't look up. Gunnar heard footsteps from his left and his right.
He heard the jangling of a collar to his left.
The thwack, thwack, thwack of laces hitting boots on his right.

"Hino, tell your men to listen. Tell them if Mörder can heel, they should know how to as well."

"Mein Anführer, ihre Ohren sind noch neu, gib mir deine Befehle und ich werde ihren Erfolg sicherstellen," Hino's head was bowed, eyes staring at Gunnar's steel-toed boots.
They were so polished that Hino saw the worry in his eyes reflected in the leather.

"Gehörlose Hunde hören keine Kugeln" Gunnar stared at the White Laces, furious. They still hadn't looked up at him.

"Fang einen Affen am schwanz und bring ihn hierher zurück." Gunnar roared at the top of his lungs.
The white laces heads turned in unison toward the darkened barroom, smiles creeping across their faces.

"Sag wahr?" one asked.

"Welche Art?" the other chirped.

"Ein Beispiel," Gunnar barked.
The White Laces didn't hesitate. They looked at Hino. He nodded, and they jogged out the door and up the sidewalk, past Rainbow's. If Gunnar wanted an example of what a blight on humanity the Affen were, they knew just who to capture by the tail.

Didi watched as the two boys ran past her in the darkened doorway and into the bodega.
She felt the sun hitting the toes of her shoes, and she thought about the $200 in her pocket.
Didi got up and began walking toward the C.

As the White Laces put six Cobra Tall Boys on the counter, they saw the Schwarzer Affe they had in mind walking toward the train.

"Ooh, ooh, ooh."

"Ooh. Ooh. Ooh!"
Didi could hear two voices making monkey noises on the sidewalk behind her. She remembered how her friend told her

to get out of town before he gave her more money at once than she had seen in a decade. Didi crossed Frederick Douglass Boulevard and descended into the 116th street C station headed downtown as her kinky black head disappeared underground.

Gunter, the White Lace holding the black plastic bodega bag barked, "catch her by the tail before she catches a train!"

Both boys crossed Frederick Douglass in four long strides, turned down the stairs on the South side, and descended like bats into hell. They leapt the stiles in tandem, one searching up the platform, one down. Didi watched from the landing halfway up the Northside stairs as they disappeared in both directions and ran back to the street just as the M10 bus pulled away.

Didi hadn't known what these men had been doing this morning. "Planning a picnic," she thought. "*Or something like that,*" she said, and ran headlong toward Morningside Park.

Gunter came back up the north stairs alone. "Sitz, bleib, guter Hund," he had said to Lukas. He had left him half the cobras and told him to see if any other prey turned up.

Gunter trotted West to Morningside Park. He knew Crackheads and Junkie Monkeys hang out in the harder to reach places. Maybe he'd find a Schwarzer Affe wandering away from its tribe.

Didi had been attacked before, tricked into going somewhere
she didn't have any business being.
Somewhere she shouldn't have been.
Traded touchin' for beer or liquor *or somethin' like that* more
times than she could remember even if she had been sober and
medicated for a decade.

She climbed the stairs toward Columbia, thinking about all of
the other times she'd gotten in too deep, running out of steam
and oxygen with every step.

She reached the top and looked down toward the bottom.

One of those boys had followed her.
He stood at the bottom and looked like he was waving at her,
or *somethin' like that.*

Once again and totally exhausted, Didi ran.

As Dolores "Didi" Dunkley begged God to help her find the
strength to fight if she needed to and to run as long as she
could, the air filled with the sound of a church bell peeling.

At #53 W 116th in Apartment 7, David looked at his reflection
in the bathroom mirror. He was only 20 years old, but felt like
the 76 Adolf Erichsen had been. Gray soot and ash had swirled
on the bathtub floor before disappearing into the drain leaving
the smell of smoke, kerosene, and burning wood behind for a

moment. He stared at his chest. Two years ago he had been a little boy who was attacked one night and known none of this. Now he had muscles, had fully shaved and regrown his hair five times, and depending on the city he was last seen at a Dog Whistle in, had Green, Hazel, or Brown eyes. He'd only not worn colored lenses in Chicago. He thought he'd only have to smoke out one viper pit. He'd thought about how wrong he'd been, how he'd lived and shuffled between Tulsa, Austin, Orlando, Chicago and now Harlem.

David heard the bells ring out a second time.

He realized he was trapped in here until 8:00 PM.

Didi pulled herself along the trailway tucked under Morningside Avenue.

Eyes searching for anywhere to hide.

A third bell.

Gunter ran up the stairs as he watched the Jezebel sprint into the underbrush ahead.

The clock rang a fourth.

At #47 on 116th Rainbow got the mail early.

Three envelopes, one from the Butcher, one from CON-ED, one from Amex.

All red.

Rainbow looked at the empty dining room.

Not one lunch customer.

The bells cried out for a fifth time.
In the 116th Street subway station Lukas, the other White
Lace, sat silently where Gunter had left him. He cracked one of
the three cobras he had open and thought he heard church
bells as the Northbound train arrived.

At the top of Morningside Park, Didi Dunkley dove into a
space under a Manhattan Juniper tree she slept beneath
sometimes when it rained or when one of her man friends
wanted to go somewhere private, or somethin' like that.
Didi heard the bell peel and whispered to herself, "seven, seven,
go to heaven."

In the Biergarten at #45, Gunnar heard the bells start.
He had counted as he stared at tonight's cross and the picnic
table beyond that.
        "Eins, zwei, drei, vier funf, sechs, sieben," and then
Gunnar Erichsen closed his eyes and began to weep before
yelling out, "ACHT! ACHT! ACHT! HEIL! HEIL! HEIL!"

Gunter had seen the Affe go into the tree as his ears filled with
rings seven, eight, and nine.
        Ten.
Gunter crouched.
        Eleven.
Gunter reached, his hands out, ready to pull.
        Twelve.
Dolores Dunkley felt something grab and yank her leg, felt her
head hit the cold ground and all the lights went out.

Or somethin' like that.

When she woke up 8 hours later, tied to a table looking up at the night sky and a bonfire attended by ghosts, Didi would wonder why she hadn't listened to her friend this morning, or somethin' like that.

Rainbow sat at the front counter until 12:30.
At 12:28, she saw two skinheads run past the dining room window toward the bar.
At 12:29, she saw them run back the way they had come, this time carrying zip ties and a German Shepherd on a chain leash. And with that, she thought of the cross in the backyard of #45, looked at the red bills in front of her and walked outside. She pulled the sandwich board and hung the sign in the window that said, **"on a smoke break, we'll reopen for dinner!"** and locked the door.
Rainbow looked around the empty restaurant and walked to the basement door. She heard a noise coming from below, A scratching, squeaking high pitched noise.
        "Rats." Rainbow said to herself as she flicked the switch to the stair lights and began her descent into madness. She heard the sound of a rat in a box, tipped the lid open and saw a little gray head look up at her as she slammed the lid shut and screamed.
Rainbow walked to the far wall and there in the darkened corner, was the ax Granddaddy Freeman had started this whole place with. Rainbow picked up the axe, the metal head

scraping the poured concrete floor. She walked back to the squeaking box, thought about pulling it open again, and then kicked it. The box bounced off her shoe, tipped forward, the flap thwacked to the floor. Rainbow braced herself. She pulled the axe up over her head.

"Pretend it's a chicken." She said to herself as she saw a little pink nose begin to appear.

"No," she heard herself say. "Pretend it's that *Rat* next door."

Rainbow brought the axe down perfectly, splitting the little rat's head from its body cleanly. She watched the small head bounce and roll under the big shelf Granddaddy Freeman had built almost 100 years ago as a pool of blood washed the cardboard box in a dark purple-red goo.

"Goddamn it," Rainbow groaned as she saw the head disappear into the darkness.

She sighed, sat the axe against the wall, and began to climb the stairs in search of a flashlight.

She reached the kitchen and saw the Kit Kat clock roll his eyes. As the clock ticked to 12:45, Rainbow searched the entire kitchen for her silver Maglite to no avail.

She climbed the stairs to her apartment and began opening drawers and slamming them shut when she came up empty. *Then she remembered where it was.*

Rainbow walked into her darkened bedroom, bands of light illuminating the edges of her pulled curtains. She saw it then, on the small table by her window, she remembered how it had gotten up here.

How she had shown it into the "Biergarten" last month when they lit their cross. How she wanted Gunnar to know that a loogie wasn't going to scare her off, even if he felt bold enough to humiliate her at the opera.

He was darkness and fire.
She was smoke and light.

She remembered how she had waited to make sure he was looking up at her, those horribly even teeth smiling up at her window. How she had quoted Dr. King as she put her hand on the power button.

"Darkness cannot drive out Darkness. Only Light can do that," and lit up Gunnar's face in dim white light.

She remembered how he pulled his arm up over his eyes and turned away when the beam hit his retinas.
She hadn't slept that night, afraid she would hear breaking glass downstairs.

Then she remembered the rat in the basement's body draining of blood on the box flap head somewhere under a shelf. Rainbow picked up the Maglite and went back down, first to the kitchen for a set of tongs in case the head was too far back to reach. She looked over her shoulder at the clock, Its hands indicating 1:05.

Rainbow stepped back into the basement, hoping against hope that she didn't vomit when she located the head.

At 1:06, Gunter and Lukas had finished jogging back to
Morningside Park. They had gotten the unconscious Affe up
the staircase to Morningside Drive and were sitting on a bench,
ignoring joggers, day walkers and even two police officers. They
saw a Mercedes-Benz pull up to the curb in front of them and
the back gate swing open as Hino came around the driver side.
        "Wirf es nach hinten," Hino snarled.
The two White Laces lifted Didi's unconscious body by the
shoulders, and hoisted her into the cargo area.

Just before 1:30 Rainbow on her hands and knees, tongs in one
hand, Maglite in the other, found the little rat's head.
It was resting on the baseboard at the back of the shelf.
For two minutes after shining her light on it, Rainbow
wretched and dry heaved.

        When she finally put herself together She chanted,
"Pretend it's a chicken head, Judith. Just a chicken head that
rolled away on accident."

She bent down again, pressed her ear to the floor, closed the
tongs together twice, and inhaled.
She relaxed her grip as the jaws of the tongs mawed open.
Rainbow jutted the tongs forward.
She felt them first press against, then into, then through
something waxy but firm.

She felt as the tongs tore through the baseboard, her hands trained by thousands of hours at the smoker and in the dining room serving Sunday supper, clenched.

The rein of the tongs closed and pulled whatever was in them back toward herself in the basement light.
Rainbow looked down inside the gob of old newspapers, beeswax, and paint chips.
Somewhere in there, a dead rat's head.
She knew it was by the way one onyx black eye and pinky gray ear popped out at her like it had just heard a noise a moment before.

But between the tong and the eye projected in the beam of the Maglite, backlit like Mount Sinai at the top of Morningside Park were five teeth.
Three incisors and two canines.

Rainbow, who had wretched and heaved moments before, vomited all over the rat, the tongs and the teeth.

Rainbow felt the timer in her pocket go off.
Time to check the smoker, time to flip meat nobody was buying. Meat she couldn't afford, even if she threw a whole month of Social Security at it.
She had used most of her May and June checks to pay July's property taxes, and then thought about how she wouldn't be able to pay in October if nothing changed.

Rainbow looked down again at the now vomit covered mass. She threw up again.

Rainbow pulled herself up, grabbing the shelves as she did. She noticed peeling paint at the back, thought of the tongs in her hand and tossed it across the room.

Rainbow pulled the corner of her apron to her mouth, wiped, let it fall, then pulled the loop over her neck, undid the waist tie and tossed the apron in the utility bin.

She put her hand on the railing and felt the back up timer go off.

At 2:05, Judith Jefferson just about jumped out of her skin.

She began to climb. Her foot settled on the first step, and it let out a haunted squeak.
"JESUS CHRIST!" Rainbow screamed out before laughing her way back into the sunlight.

Didi thought she heard someone yell "Jesus Christ" or somethin' like that. She blinked twice, the sun scalding her eyes. Didi tried to raise her arm to shield her eyes and realized she couldn't.
"Hello? Hello?" Didi cried loud in case someone was outside near her.
"ooh ooh ooh," two voices called in low voices.

Didi felt two hands pull her mouth open and then saw another arm blot out the sun.
Hot liquid flooded Didi's mouth, the taste of watered down cheap beer washing over her tongue, then pouring up her nose, into her eyes and pooling in her ears and hair. She began to gag and choke, burping sprays of the beer into the air and across her neck and chest.

Dolores 'Didi' Dunkley watched as a new hand momentarily appeared, holding something else before jamming it, whatever it was, into her mouth. She felt all four hands let go, then two pulled her head up by the hair.

The thing still jammed against her uvula.

She heard the unmistakable sound of duct tape peeling off the roll, and then the gummy edge stuck to the nape of her neck. She watched the sun disappear and reappear half a dozen times before she felt her head tug to the side, the sound of the tape ripping off the roll muffled by the layers of it over her ears, the other hands letting go again.
Didi felt the waxy, slick skin of an unpeeled banana on her teeth as it cut off her air and her tongue spasmed beneath it.

"Willst du eine banane, Tante?" A third man's voice asked before all three voices broke into laughter.

Dolores Dunkley heard the sound of buckets rattling.

She watched as the perfectly round bottom of one eclipsed the sun entirely.

She felt something hit her thighs and belly.
At that moment, she realized she was totally nude.

She heard the voices saying something and then felt the banana clog her airway entirely.

The sun began to reappear as Didi felt herself start to choke to death.

She watched as a strange red rain began to fall from the bucket above her head in clumps and balls.

As her body began to convulse, realizing there was no air or help coming, her vision filled with the tiny feet and giant mandibles of fire ants, their bites lighting her skin on fire as the light in her eyes died.

Behind the privacy fence dividing #47 from the horror show next door, Rainbow jammed her thermometer in and out of a brisket, 1/2 rack of ribs, and then a Cornish hen she had found deep in the freezer but still within date. She thought about the teeth and the wall and the rat's head. *Whose teeth were they? How long had they been there? How would they get there?*

Rainbow looked at the rear window above the stairs and thought about Daddy and Mama, about Granny Caledonia, about Granddaddy Freeman.

Which of them had done this?

Rainbow glazed the half rack of ribs and closed the door to the smoker.

She checked her watch, 2:15.

Rainbow set her timer for 60 minutes and went back inside, considering what to do with the basement, the rat, the tongs, and the teeth.

Beyond the other side of the fence, ants danced across Dolores "Didi" Dunkley's body in the afternoon sun. Gunter and Lukas stared at the red wave washing forward and back on her warm brown skin.

"Handrechen, Spaten, Handjäter. Wie Silberbesteck," Hino yapped at them in *beschissen* Dutch. He saw their eyes glaze over and said, "hand rake, spade, hand weeder. Like silverware."

The two White Laces began laying all the gardening tools on the two picnic benches.

In the darkened barroom, Gunnar Erichsen sent his sister an email.

"Schwarzes Blut wurde vergossen. Nehmen Sie das rote Auge mit nach Hause und beenden Sie, was Sie heute Morgen begonnen haben."

Rainbow took almost two hours to clean up the dead rat, vomit and tongs. As she tied the handle of the trash bag and began to climb the stairs again, she realized she had forgotten the smoker. She tossed the bag in the trash, slammed down the lid, and pulled the door open. Billows of smoke poured into the mid afternoon air. The ribs covered in a thick black crust, the brisket peeling and cracking, and the once light brown game hen now a smoky, shiny gray.

Rainbow went into the kitchen and got a tray and fresh set of tongs. She piled the burned meat high and went back inside. She tossed the tray on the metal prep table, looked at the ribs smoldering still, then the basement door.
She pulled a side drawer open and grabbed a pair of gardening gloves.

Rainbow looked at the clock.
Just before 4:30.

Rainbow turned and went into the basement and pulled everything from the bottom shelf. She piled cans and containers along the base of the stairs. When she realized the upper shelves would need to be emptied too, she got a step stool.
Rainbow checked her watch, 5:55, make a wish.
She wished anyone had knocked on the door today.
She wished whatever was behind the shelf was piles of money or gold bars.

Rainbow looked up the stairs, then at the empty shelf. She decided to tie a rope to the top and pull it down. She didn't even know where to begin sliding it out without it falling on her. This way she could at least jump behind the water heater if she needed to. Rainbow looped the rope behind one arm of the shelf, ran it across and around the other. She put one end of the rope in her gloved right hand, the other in her left and walked backward until the rope pulled taut.
She took a deep breath and yanked with all her might.
The bells of Saint John the Divine began ringing out.
With the first toll the shelf wobbled.
With the second, it rocked forward.
As the sound of the third bell came down the basement stairs, the sound of a crashing shelf peeled back up toward the street. A great cloud of dust covered the basement air.

David woke up to the sound of the fourth ring.
He slept from 17:40 to 18:00 like a true Ubermensch in training.

As the fifth and sixth bells rang out, Rainbow saw where the wall had been cut away and filled back in.

David rose from his twin bed and dropped to the floor.
His back and arms raised and lowered 87 times.
He laid on the floor and began sitting up and back down 87 times.
He stood up and jumped, body extending into giant Xes, 87 times.

David went into the bathroom and turned the shower on.

The water was as cold as it could get.

For 8 minutes he shivered and washed his body.

His Vagus nerve sent signals to panic as he told his mind to remain calm.

David turned in the bathroom mirror, feeling muscle pull against scar tissue.

He thought again about those first three Dog Whistlers, about Val, about Tulsa and Austin and Chicago and Orlando.

**

He had flown into Orlando one minute before midnight, and gone to the Walmart. He bought two cans of kerosene, a pack of wool socks, a bundle of nylon rope, and a plastic container of apple and almond strudel. He had paid in cash, wore a ball cap and fake glasses, and walked two blocks back to his car, taking five blocks to get there.

At 2:01 AM "Werner" called Adolf Erichsen.

"Heil, Adolf. Brauchen Sie Hilfe?"

He handed Adolf and Elka fresh cups of coffee at 4:45 AM and opened the strudel.

For 10 minutes they ate and drank.

Then, two thuds rang out.

Adolf and Elka face down in their pastries.

He had dragged their chairs to the center of the Biergarten against tonight's cross and tied them both up, robes and all. He slid the socks over their hands and then put their hoods on backward and sat down against the Falu Red wall and waited for them to come around.

At 5:50am, they both did just that.

"Was ist das?" Adolf murmured.

"Lass mich hier raus!" Elka wailed.

They both began thrashing, trying to break loose of their bonds.

They heard a voice almost like the boy they knew as Werner say, "Deine Tochter hat meine Mutter getötet. Jetzt werde ich dich töten, dann seine Eltern, dann sie und ihn."

"No, no, please, please," they both cried.

David picked up their cell phones and scrolled their contacts. There were only four in both.

Self, Adolf or Elka depending, and two more, both the same Sohn and Tochter.

He pressed one of each and hit the green button.

He held the one ringing Tochter to his ear.

He heard Evangeline's voice say, "Mutter? Hallo?" before he lit a match and held it to the rest of the book. It fizzled and sizzled to life in his hand.

He tossed it to the feet of Adolf Erichsen and heard him, and then Elka began to scream.

He heard Evangeline yelling into the phone.

Then he heard *The Voice* yelling in the background.

Elka Erichsen yelled, "Geschwister! Nicht verheiratet!" Every word he had planned gone just like that.

David was speechless.

**

"Take a deep breath and calm your nerves," Rainbow said to herself, staring at the moldy, torn edges of the bottom corner of the fake wall. Her eye followed the line where the real plaster became the amalgam of newspaper, beeswax, body parts and white paint. She pulled the gloves down around her wrists, and stepped between the spaces the now horizontal shelf had made. A pathway toward an 88 year old mystery that Freeman Jefferson hoped nobody would ever find. Rainbow punched the wall, hoping she was right. Chunks of the wall around her hand fell to the floor. She punched again. Again. She felt all her rage built up over the course of the last seventeen months let loose. She punched and clawed and dug the entire false wall into rubble. She could see bits of human bone, more teeth, clumps of blonde hair, clumps of brown hair, and then in the bottom of it all, wrapped in a mappine, a small recipe box. The top had two things on it. The word LONG and the drawing of a pig.

Rainbow climbed through the slats of the shelves back toward the stairs and tiptoed her way through the cans and bottles littering the floor. She ignored the squeak of the first step, walked past the tray of burnt meat, and pulled a chair back from a table, took her gloves off and set the box in front of her. Rainbow watched as a boy who looked like David pressed his face to the glass, not seeing her in the half slack of the shade. She saw the boy's Hazel eyes dart around and then pull away and head East toward number 45.
Rainbow turned and looked at the clock, the Kit Kats eyes leering back and then darting the other direction.

His belly read, 7:55.
*Had she really been down there beating the wall to smithereens
that long?*

She turned back to the box, put her hand on the lid, and pulled
it open.
A small stack of index cards hid inside.

David looked at his reflection of the pulled shade of the dining
room window as he strode past it, his hair perfectly slicked
back, his shoulders broad and square. He blinked twice as his
vision tinged brown and green before resettling. He reached in
his pocket and pulled out the matchbook Gunnar, The Voice,
had given him.

He greeted the man at the door timidly. He'd done this part
four times before.
       "Hi. A man. You probably know him, well, maybe not.
Anyway, is this? Am I? Am I in the right place?" He unfolded
his hand and revealed the red dog whistle on the cover.
       "First time, kid?" every bouncer at every Dog Whistle
had said it the same way.
       "I yeah, I'm sick of seeing affirmative action let people
like O-Bummer think he could lead a nation," David had
learned saying 'O-Bummer' made the bouncer or bartender or
other attendees giggle and drop their guard.
The bouncer pulled a chain from under his collar. At the end
of it was a red dog whistle.

David watched as the bouncer put his lips to it and blew, his
cheeks puffing out as he did.
David scrunched his face up like he was trying to listen.

"Don't worry kid, only dogs can hear it. That and
well-heeled Laces."

"What's a Lace?"

"You'll see. Lots to learn and tonight's a special one.
Got a 'pick-a-nick' out back just for tonight."
The bouncer opened the door and led David inside.
Where a coat check would be was a woman wearing a Klan
robe with no hood.

"First time, it's all over your face. Take this and put it
on. Allows for you to react without anyone seeing you smile."
The woman did just that, revealing the tar stained teeth and a
space where her bottom right incisor had been.

"I, I didn't realize this was still a, a, well, forgive me, a
thing." David could do this first night coy-boy song and dance
in his sleep.
Next she'd ask his size.
He'd say medium.
She'd say large to hide his boots.

"Is there a fee or a donation?"

"No, you just tell me a size," she said.

"Medium." David waited.

"Take a large, it'll cover your boots in case you're on the
train home with someone here."
David pulled the robe over his head and felt as it tumbled to
the floor around him. He thought about how all the people in

these bars looked like racist princesses in Lily-White gowns and
laughed as he pulled the hood on.
He was swallowed by darkness.
He heard the woman laugh and he began to panic,
remembering the way his day had begun.
He felt a hand tug at the chin of his hood.
He felt his hair pull against the fabric.
Then he saw a light appear, first in one eye, then the other.
He saw the woman reaching up at his face and laughing.
	"Didn't know where you went for a second, did ya?"
She asked and laughed again.
	"You got me straightened out though," he said.
	"Not yet I didn't. Go out back, pick a picker, and let
your anger out with everyone else playing, 'Pick the Nigger' it's
one of our oldest traditions for venting frustrations at the
Affe."
David's stomach did a somersault.

He glanced around the barroom, folding chairs in rows facing a
platform and dais.
An American Flag and Swastika hung in the back.
He saw a few dogs, mainly Shäferhund and Pit Bulls.

David walked into the Biergarten and his stomach flipped
again.
He stared at a cross and beyond that, a table with a red and
white cloth and something large and dark brown on top of
that.

David stepped closer, and through the eye holes saw a body covered in bright red bite marks from some kind of bug. David watched as a dozen hands picked up spades and weeders and hand rakes. He watched as a woman picked up a scythe and dragged it along one of the legs, a trickle of blood forming as she went. He watched a hand pick up a hand weeder and drive it full force into the body's side.

The body began bouncing around, groaning under the tape around Its mouth.

It clutched and grabbed at the tablecloth.

David walked toward the head.

He saw great swollen eyelids fluttering wildly, the eyes inside them bouncing back and forth like Rainbow's Kit Kat Klock.

"I thought you said she was dead?!" a voice cried.

"She was!" another voice yelled.

"Mmmphh phhmmm..." The body looking up at David, said. His brain heard the lilt of the body's voice. David's brain ran the voice through his head.

"Mmmphh phmmm," it said.

"Myyy frienddd," David's brain played back.

A hooded figure pulled out a piece of duct tape and pressed it against the body's nose. It began to bounce and beat against the table.

"Moment Mal," David heard Gunnar's voice say.

David watched the body wriggle and squirm.

He heard voices from all the hoods begin to howl and whoop, "OOH! OOH! OOH!"

And as the still somehow alive body of Didi Dunkley fought for the last time, the crowd drove their tools into her flesh and tore her apart in stabs and slices and sprays of blood and guts.

David felt his stomach rocket its contents up his throat and out his mouth and nose and onto the inside of his hood.
And then, for the first time since June two years ago, David fainted with Nazis all around him.

At 8:08, Rainbow saw the street lights illuminate the vinyl shades covering the window and door. She turned the eight index cards over and over in her hands. Each had tips on preparation, cooking duration and suggestions on how to make the presentation 'look natural.' There was a card titled 'Adam's Ribs' with instructions to create an apple wine sauce. One titled 'Sweet Breads and Sweet Cheeks' that suggested a casserole dish for maintaining juices and moisture. She flipped past a recipe for Rump Roast and one for 'Daddy's Links' before looking at her favorite, 'Brisket by the Basket.' At the bottom of the box, she found a note written in a woman's hand. Rainbow carried the note with her to the front door to check the lock. To the back door to do the same. She held it as she looked at the tray of cold burnt meat and fought the urge to gag. She wrapped the note around the handle of the Maglite and turned the downstairs lights off and made her way up the front stairs and into the darkened living room. Rainbow pulled the Afghan off the back of the sofa, wrapped it around herself, clicked on the flashlight and began to read.

In the Biergarten of #45 Gunnar pulled the hood off the
Klansman on the ground's face and slapped him gently awake.
As David opened his eyes, he felt the cool night air on his
cheeks and forgot for a moment where he was.

"First picnic can be a little rough," Gunnar's voice said
from above. "Hoped I'd see you last month, but nothing like
going from the frying pan straight into the fire."
A hand reached down, and David grabbed it. His vision swirled
sideways, then right side up, Didi's desecrated corpse spilling
off the table and onto the grass, the dogs lapping it up.

"First meeting, first picnic, first faint. I'd say *that*
deserves to be the first match of the night," Gunnar said.
David remembered throwing the first match just before 6:15
this morning and almost fainted again. He tottered. Gunnar
caught him under the arm.

"First match?" David asked, like he'd never heard of
fire.
David lit his match, held it to the rows of White match heads
and watched as they smoked for a half second, then exploded to
life, one after the other.
David threw the matchbook at the cross. It erupted in flames.
They licked their way up and across the kerosene soaked wood.
David saw Didi's illuminated corpse in the firelight.

"Jetzt bin ich zum Tod geworden, Zerstörer der
Welten," David felt his mouth say as fresh black smoke filled
the air and his nose.

David thought about his friend Didi and how he had tried to save her, wondered why she hadn't listened, and then thought of this morning.

Adolf and Elka Erichsen face down in a strudel.

He thought of how they had screamed in the darkness of the hoods and burned to death.

David felt something inside him burst, like an overfull dam.

He stared into the fire and began to laugh as he thought about the whole day.

He heard the robes around him start laughing too, as they all rode the sounds of fire crackling and his uncontrollable titters into mania.

At 21:30, the Klansman sat enrobed elbow to enrobed elbow and listened to the overture of Wagner's Rienzi come to a crescendo.

David remembered the loogie and got nauseous again.

"Heute ist Acht, Acht, Acht. Heil Hitler!" Gunnar's voice boomed across the wave of eyeholes.

"Acht!" Acht! Acht! Heil! Heil! Heil!" the hoods all chanted back.

"Today was supposed to be historic. Today was," Gunnar paused and cleared his throat, "There is a rat in the house."

The crowd began to murmur to themselves.

"SCHWEIGEN." Gunnar bellowed.

The eyeholes, wherever they were looking, snapped back to their Grand Dragon.

"I will say this in English so new brothers and sisters will all understand me," Gunnar's chest puffed out, "for the safety of all of us, anonymity inside these walls is no longer an option. This morning our bar in Orlando was torched. Evangeline is not here tonight because she is there touring the scene. One of our members was there when two men broke down the door. Our member dispatched one with his Luger, but the other escaped. He, unfortunately, is White. Now, we don't savor culling our own herd, but clearly this Buck thinks race-mixing is worth killing for."

The crowd booed and hissed under their hoods like displeased snakes.

Gunnar reached his point, "Because he could be anyone, and because Orlando is only a few hours away, tonight before we conclude our festivities I kindly ask that you take your hoods off."

The crowd of eyeholes began to glance around. Then David saw his chance to earn his way inside. He stood and faced the room.

"Heil. My name is Max."

"Max had never been here before tonight. You may remember him from having a moment of overwhelming excitement earlier," Gunnar said, both of them remembering how "Max" had fainted.

"I didn't put a new hood on after that, because I saw the strength and purity of this realm's Grand Dragon and knew I'd be safe out there in," David paused, trying to stick the landing.

Gunnar cut him off, "Out there in the jungle with the Affen," the crowd applauded.
A few men revealed their faces.

"By the end of the year, Haarlem will once again be a Whitopia. Unmask yourselves and say hello to your True neighbors," Gunnar concluded. One by one, every mask came off. 87 ugly White faces including Gunnar. 88 including Max. A cuckoo clock popped out of the little chalet on the wall. It called out 10 times before disappearing again.

"Gute Nacht, Heil Hitler." Gunnar barked as he raised his arm to 45 degrees and walked through the open faced crowd.

At 10:10, Max walked down to the 110th Street stop, stood against the bulletin board on the center platform, and listened for a Northbound train while watching for a Southbound one and any Klansman who were in attendance. At 10:13, he got on a 3 and rode it all the way up to 148th Street before catching a 2 down to 110th again and walking an extra long way home so he didn't have to pass the block that Didi would never sit on again.

At 11:47, he was finally home.
And twenty-four hours after his day had begun, David fell asleep, deeply and uninterrupted until morning.

**

At 7:10pm West Coast time, Evangeline Erichsen stepped off a plane in Portland.

At 7:55 local time, she entered Erichsen's Koffee Shop.

At 8:58, when everyone else was outside, Evangeline pulled the gas lines off the stoves.

At 9:30 she spoke about the importance of sacrifice for the many.

At 9:35, she handed everyone a cigar but asked that they not light them till she left.

  She told the crowd, "ich bin schwanger," and walked to her rental at the far end of the lot.

At 9:37, as she reapplied her Falu lipstick, she felt the car shake and alarms around the parking lot go off.

She looked in the mirror.

She hadn't smeared her lipstick.

She hadn't flinched.

At 10:43pm she handed a gate attendant her ticket and boarded a plane back to Newark.

At 7:53 AM on August 9th, Evangeline Erichsen turned the key to the apartment door. She said Guten Morgen to Mörder, Gunnar's dog, and pulled a raw swordfish steak out of the fridge and tossed it into a large kennel in the bathroom.

  "Guten Morgen, Pistenraupe," a deep caterwaul came from the darkened bathroom. Evangeline saw Gunnar sitting on the sofa, staring at the morning outside. "Soll ich jetzt das gift aussaugen, Bruter?" She asked.

  "Ja, wie Mama es dir beigebracht hat," he answered. Evangeline kneeled in front of Gunnar and slid down his shorts. She caressed his *schwanz*, put it in her mouth, and

began to suck. She thought about how she had suggested this
26 hours ago, before Mutter and Vater died, and the day that
followed. She thought of how much she loved her brother,
how he had led the meeting here last night. Bravely ignoring his
grief. She thought about how a woman's work is truly never
done, and for two hours she milked Gunnar, her husband, her
brother, her Ubermensch, bone dry the way Mutter had made
her practice on Vater, langsam und mit Liebe, als sie ein Kleines
Mädchen war.

Chapter Fifteen

5/1/2007: The Price of Freedom

"But now they stand in a rusty row, all empty,
because the L&N don't stop here anymore."

~Johnny Cash, "The L&N don't stop here anymore"

On April 21st, 2007, Lisa had left lunch with
Rainbow and called her lawyer. Both Carol, her attorney, and
the head partner at the firm, Barry, told her there was nothing
anyone could do. Matthew could have let them open for free if
he wanted, and as far as the duffel bag of cash was concerned, it
was hearsay.

They had both apologized and Barry said, "Lisa, a
Neo-Nazi bar on 116th has as good a chance of survival as a
two headed calf born in the middle of the night. By morning
something comes along and kills it, or death naturally comes to
a thing that makes no sense."

Dissatisfied, she pulled out her brave and polite voice and
dialed Matthew himself.

"Hello, Matthew, how are you? Listen, I need help
with an inspection at one of the units on 136th. Can you come
with me? You know how scary that part of town is in broad
daylight? I know we're both licking our wounds, but you know
that block like I do. I've never been up there without you," Lisa
sighed and moaned the way kids do when they ask their parents
to help with something innocuous.
Matthew felt himself smile.

He'd had an idea, "Of course. How could I say *non* to
the former Mrs. Charbonneau?" Matthew winced as his own
verbal arrow nicked his spirit as it took flight.

"Back to *LeBlanc* as easily as getting ash out of white
sheets," Lisa said.

"You been to 116th lately?" Matthew asked.

Why had she said white sheets? he wondered as he listened to her.

He listened to her *tone*. It did this weird Bobby Brady thing when she lied.

"No. Why? You own 116. Remember we split our Baltic and Mediterranean Avenues up? Remember?"

Her voice hadn't changed, not even into irritation.

"When's the inspection? I'd be happy to point at the exits and pretend I know what he's talking about." Matthew thought if Lisa could be nice, so could he.

"He can come..." Lisa flipped open her day planner to May and listed the first two Tuesdays. "He can come on the 1st or the 8th."

Matthew paused. He looked at the folded towel on the small table, thought about the fat stack of cash underneath it, then looked at the small black square he'd found on the side pouch of the duffle bag, a black match book with a red dog whistle on it. He thought of how he had plans on the eighth because of it. Plans he didn't want Lisa anywhere in the neighborhood of.

"Let's do the first. I'll take you to Dinosaur BBQ." Lisa thought about Rainbow. She thought about how Matthew had apparently not just sat there while his new tenants hurled slurs at Rainbow, but he'd lied and said they belonged to her. She remembered how Rainbow had said that he left her three 50s, how he had left without a real defense or, God forbid, an honest apology. She thought about Rainbow telling her she had thrown the money away, but then decided Matthew could pay for their lunch after Lisa had seemed so concerned. She thought about the duffel bag of money and said,

"You know what, let's do it. It's a date. 2:30 on the first," then paused, took a breath in and said, "you really are a good guy Monsieur Charbonneau," as she felt her tongue try to leave her body and hung up. They had met on 136th and waited outside for 30 minutes for a man who didn't exist to show up. After what felt like an eternity, Lisa called the city inspection line and heard a woman's voice say exactly what she knew it would.

"I'm sorry ma'am, but I don't have you scheduled for today."

Lisa said thank you to the voice and hung up. She looked at Matthew and said, "Well, I guess the hard part is over. Should we go grab ribs?"
She remained calm when she asked if he'd had any interest from prospective tenants about #45, and had said there had been a few, but that they were all nervous about the neighbors.

He had called once a month after that to see if the inspector had rescheduled.
She told him "no" nine.
And then in February, a real notice came saying the pipes to the ceiling extinguisher lines in all the buildings needed to be inspected.

"Matthew, hi, it's Lisa. Can you meet me on Friday the 29th?"

"Leap Day plans. I'm jumping for joy."

The inspector said the sprinkler heads would need to be replaced next spring. All 276 of them. Every single one was more than years old. The inspector told her they're meant to last for five, especially with old pipes. She told him she'd owned the buildings for three. He said OK, signed his forms and told them both to have a nice day. Over ribs Lisa pretended she couldn't afford a million fire extinguishers, and that she, "hated even owning the buildings."
Matthew had asked if she was serious and she said maybe.

On the 8th of March 2008, at the 9th Klavern meeting, Matthew Charbonneau told his friend Gunnar that he might know of some apartments for sale if he and Evangeline wanted to get to work "truly gentrifying Haarlem".

On March 9th, 2008 Matthew called Lisa to tell her he thought he had found a buyer for the Mediterranean side of the board. They were moving here permanently from Chicago and wanted passive income. Lisa had asked if he had told them about the sprinkler caps. His voice clicked as he said yes. Lisa knew he was lying and hoped to hell that he was lying to her and didn't plan on telling these mystery buyers from Chicago.

On March 10th, 2008, Lisa LeBlanc and Judith "Rainbow" Jefferson had their eleventh Little Owl lunch, now a monthly tradition. Lisa always paid after that first lunch. Rainbow never felt guilty. As the waiter came with the check, a tray with two champagne flutes appeared. Lisa and Rainbow's plan to give

Matthew enough rope to hang himself and the Neo-Nazis next door now swinging into motion.

They clinked their glasses, sipped, and Rainbow said, "Christmas will be here before you know it."

They both drank deeply, drowning any lingering guilt about what they were going to do in a sea of bubbles.

On May 9th, 2008, Matthew called Lisa to tell her the new owners wanted to pay cash.

On May 15th, 2008, Matthew dropped off a quarter of a million dollars in five duffel bags.
He told Lisa he would give all the tenants move out notices if she gave him one duffel bag and that she'd never need to go up to 136 again if she gave him another when the final 250k was paid in July. She had thrown her arms around his neck and squeezed tight so he couldn't see her smile when she said, "of course."

When he dropped the last payment in mid-July, she gave him one of the bags and said, "take this and savor it. I think the rest of this year will be bad for just about everyone. I'm using this last payment to buy something in the Pacific Northwest, maybe Portland. I hear it's all hippies and bike rides."

She and Rainbow had their monthly Little Owl, Rainbow, barely touching her pork chop, Lisa putting her salad fork down and pushing the plate away when Rainbow told her about what she called a "Flying Dutchman".

Lisa told Rainbow how Matthew had taken the bag of cash, how sorry she was that they couldn't touch any of it until this was almost all over.

Rainbow set her fork down and stopped picking at her meat and said, "Let that Judas get his silver. It's the only way he hangs."

Chapter Sixteen

9/8/2008: Just Desserts

"Here they are again, folks! These wonderful, wonderful kids!
Still struggling! Still hoping!
As the clock of fate ticks away, the dance of destiny continues!
The marathon goes on, and on, and on!
HOW LONG CAN THEY LAST!"
~Rocky, "They Shoot Horses, Don't They?"

Rainbow heard Lisa's voice repeat itself. "Rainbow, who's Judith?"

She heard the tail of the Kit Kat kick side to side and said, "Oh, I fell asleep at the counter. Must have been dreaming about being someone else and not here."

"I missed you last month for lunch. I thought about calling but didn't want to risk one of them being—"

"Lisa. Girl. The envelopes on the mail are the same shade of red it was last month. Nobody's coming anywhere near here. Nobody's seen Didi in a month and I just know they did something to her."

"Did you see anything from the window last month?" Rainbow paused, remembering how she had heard a rat in the basement last month and found bones and recipes for how to smoke human meat in a fake wall behind a shelf in a house her grandfather, Freeman, had built 88 years ago and couldn't speak.

"Rainbow?" Lisa asked like a parrot for the third time on this phone call.

"Lisa, I'm sorry. I think I have to let you go. I'm all right. Today's just stressful. I'll see you Wednesday." Rainbow hung up and laid down on the floor of the kitchen. She tried to melt into it, let the monsters next door win and just give up. *Judith* thought about how the last time she had laid on this floor was 43 years ago, and how she wished for the same thing that night in 1965.
She closed her eyes and meditated on how she had survived that night so many years ago.

**

In the early hours of February 22nd, 1965, Rainbow had crawled out on her hands and knees; up from the basement to this floor. She remembered laying on the red and black checkerboard linoleum and felt the cool against the cuts and burns and bruises on her body from when the third man had kicked his way into the house upstairs and then kicked Rainbow in the head. He had tied her wrists together while she was unconscious. He had gone into every room, blasting down the locked bedroom door, and then dropped the black and white RCA set on Chuck Jefferson's battered head until it was unclear where the television set ended and his head began. The third drop, the one after the one that did kill Chuck, woke Rainbow up as it bounced off the massive pillowcase and Gray Matter and crashed against the floor. She felt the bindings on her wrists and tried to get to her feet. If she could get to the drawer, she could get to the knives and try to fight.

"Ooh ooh ooh," she heard from the darkness. She scrambled like a caterpillar toward the cabinets. She felt as something grabbed her feet and pulled her backward. She felt her belly slide across a slick pool of something that smelled like fried pork, and when her chin caught on the dead man's knee, she began to flail. The Goliath booted her in the stomach. She curled into a ball. He pressed his boot against her shoulder and extended his knee as hard as he could, sending Rainbow bouncing down the stairs. She landed on the backs of the knees of the other dead man and realizing she was conscious and alive, rolled toward his severed throat and slid the cleaver out from under his neck, a juicy burble of cooling blood spilling as she did. She heard as the man upstairs clomped and stomped his way down to her. She felt his shadow sweep across her back and heard drawer after drawer of spoons and tongs and spatulas and silverware fell to the floor like a rain of metal and wood. Rainbow pulled herself away from the sound on her hands and forearms, feeling her palms pull apart, blisters popping on the icy floor. A fresh wave of fire filled Rainbow's right calf as she heard the Goliath roar.

"Pick a nigger! Pick a nigger! Stick it in the thigh! Pick a nigger! Pick a nigger! Watch the nigger cry!"
He stabbed two more dinner forks in the burned and bleeding leg. He rolled her over onto her back, her dress front smeared in blood and sweat and cooled chunks of lard. She felt him pull himself against her raised knees, the handle of the fork highest up in her calf pressing against the meat of her thigh. She let out a scream of agony and fear as the Goliath socked her across the jaw, sending her head into the floor, her vision into stars, and her thoughts toward death. Judith prayed, Rainbow prayed, the woman and the woman inside the woman both, for the world to go black and let this all be over. She felt his belt buckle hit her stomach, felt him pull a handful of her skirt up, and began jamming himself against what Mama had always called her 'Daisy'.

Rainbow had only ever kissed one boy two summers before Mama got sick. Then she'd been so busy keeping her whole world afloat that she'd never gotten around to losing her 'Daisy'.

And both Judith *and* Rainbow would be Goddamned if the peckerwood honky sumbitch that killed Daddy and was trying to kill her was going to be the one to take it. Rainbow threw her hands toward her calves, pulled back the first handle she found, and drove it as hard as she could at his little White weenie. She felt it pop through what felt like raw chicken flesh and heard him yowl and felt him pop off her like a bead of water on a too hot pan.

Rainbow dropped the shucking fork in her hand and began shimmying toward the cleaver. When the third fork went into her leg, she felt her fingers grasp the handle for a moment before a bolt of force and lightning sent her sliding like a hockey puck into the proverbial net known as the basement stairs.

Rainbow slid face first down fifteen wooden stairs and onto the concrete floor, the force busting the rope around her hands free. Rainbow rolled over to look up the stairs just in time to see the Goliath hurl the cleaver at her like the first man had. She watched as the handle hit the hanging bulb, erupting the room into falling glass and near total darkness. Rainbow watched as the doorway filled with blackness as the Goliath traipsed step by step. Judith listened as the cleaver slid against the floor and hit what sounded like a bucket under the utility tub.

Rainbow's eyes and ears watched the shadow come closer and closer, chanting, "Pick a Nigger! Pick a Nigger! Put it between her thighs! Pick a Nigger! Pick a Nigger! Make sure that cunt dies!"

Rainbow watched as the shadow jiggled its pants down and began pulling on its little shadow pecker, Judith's hand found

the cleaver handle. She reached her hand up, pulled on the end of the little shadow pecker with her right hand, and pulled down on it. She felt her left hand soar like a bat through the darkness, and then the little shadow pecker was in her right hand and the rest of the shadow was yelling and running around, shouting. She stayed low, the Goliath somewhere here in the dark with her bleeding from where his pecker used to be and yelling, "I'll fucking kill you, you negra cunt!"
Rainbow got to the stairs and began walking up them backward.
As she put her heel on the fourth step she heard THUD, THOMP, THUD, THOMP, as the Goliath ran at her.
She put her arms above her head, cleaver face out.
Rainbow and Judith watched as the peckerless man came at her, and as his outstretched claws reached up for the blade.
She brought it down as hard and fast as she'd ever hoped to again.
His thumbs both popped off of his hands, two arcs of blood shooting into the darkness.
He let out a final half roar as the cleaver embedded itself in the space between his eyes.
He stumbled forward, the cleaver ding-dinging against the stairs.

**

"Ding, Ding."
Rainbow opened her eyes.
Kitchen floor, 2008.

"Hello? Hello, can we get some service?" A woman's voice was calling from out front. Rainbow looked at the Kit Kat clock, 5:27. She pulled herself to her feet, brushed her hands on her apron, and stepped into the dining room.

A family of four was standing at the doorway, A mom, dad, teenage boy and little girl, all blonde with blue eyes.

"Finally, you'd think for an almost dead business, you'd be a little quicker with the service." The woman clucked at Rainbow.

"I'm so sorry, ma'am. I was checking the smoker out back. Don't normally get customers till about six. You folks go ahead and pick a seat. I'll grab you all some water and menus." Rainbow didn't recall the last time a four-top was in.

"Well, to tell the truth, we saw the 8 for $8 sign outside and didn't think you'd be in here," the husband said flatly.

Rainbow looked to the family, confused.

"88. You cook next door to the only Kwality Klavern in New York City and don't know 88?" This time it was the teen boy.

"Have a seat, please. I'll grab the menus and then you can tell me what 88 means." Rainbow felt her right calf get warm.

"Hail Hitler, you dumb monkey," The boy spat.

"Oh, see, I'm glad you know. It means you must also know I'm who rented this space to the boys next door. My granddaddy opened this joint almost 100 years ago. My daddy ran it and now me. But you see the junkies out there on the corner. I want the good old days back."

Did she really expect them to believe that?

"See, honey? This one knows her place," the husband said to the wife before looking at Rainbow and continuing, "We moved up from Tulsa. Oklahoma coons remember what happened. They stay in line like you do. We'll eat here, just wear gloves. And I better not find any of them kinky hairs in the sauce."

"Lawds no, Sir. Hygienic and clean as Black hands can be." Rainbow had to keep herself from soft shoeing or slitting her wrists right there and then. "I'm gonna fetch that water."

She heard three chairs pull out and push in. She listened to a little girl clap the table and stomp on a dining chair her granddaddy Freeman bought almost 100 years ago as she heard the mom say in a lilting voice,

"Can you say *Affen*?"
After the little girl said it, Rainbow put four cups on her tray, spit in each, and then put two vinyl gloves on before filling them.

She heard the mom say, "this is BBQ, but tonight we're going to a pick-a-nick!"
She heard the girl and boy clap and woo. Her skin crawled imagining what a 'pick-a-nick' looked like next door. She saw her shining silver metal meat mallet on the silver prep table next to the cleaver. She walked back into the dining room holding the tray high.

"Four waters poured with my gloves on. I'm going to check the smoker and come get your orders," Rainbow said.

"We'll need menus first," the wife glowered.

"I am so sorry again, ma'am, I don't know where my head is at.

"Probably wishing we were your people so you didn't have to speak proper English."

"You'ze, sorry, you are completely correct. I'm sorry, it's so bright in here. Do you mind if I draw the shade?"

"Please, seeing those Junkie Monkeys out there is ruining my appetite," the shithead son said.
Rainbow walked to the window and pulled the shade, looped the pull around a nail in the sill so it wouldn't roll back up, and excused herself to the kitchen.

She pulled three menus and heard the little girl go "Ooh! Ooh!" and then the mother say, "verrry good. That's the sound an Affe makes!"

Rainbow went to the island and put the meat mallet in her apron pocket and walked back into her current Hell. She handed the menus out one by one. Not a single thank you. Not a look up, not a clearing throat; until the little one looked her dead in the eye and went, "ooh ooh, ooh, Affe! ooh, ooh!"

And when all three of the others laughed, she smiled and said, "I'm sorry, I forgot to introduce myself, I'm *Judith*."

The father looked up and said, "we're the Jorgensens," and Rainbow smiled.

"Mr. Jorgensen, excuse me one moment I thought I saw someone at the door." Rainbow walked to the front door, opened it, looked up and down the block and heard a voice from over her shoulder ask,

"Can you close it? The Goddamn zoo is so loud."

"Of course." She closed the door and locked it in one fluid motion. "Let me turn on some ambient music to drown it out totally." Rainbow walked to a shelf behind Mrs. Jorgensen, turned on the stereo and hit play.

The tinkling melody of Donna Fargo began, *"Do you love waking up next to me as much as I love waking up next to you?"*

Rainbow put her hand in her apron and clenched the handle of the mallet. "Do you know what Sweetbreads are, Mister Jorgenson?"

"Well, I can't say I do," Mr. Jorgensen said.

"Isn't it, brains, dad?" The boy asked. new

"Nobody would eat brains, Addie," Mrs. Jorgensen said.

"Oh no?" Rainbow locked eyes with Mr. Jorgensen.

"Wait, wait..." Mr. Jorgensen's eyes went wide as he saw the mallet arc through the air like two silver rainbows. One going out; one swinging, strong and clean back, ending its journey at the back right corner of Mrs. Jorgensen's scalp before a pot of golden hair, crimson blood and gray and Nigra launched across the wall.

"See? Black in every brain." Rainbow brought the hammer up to swing on the shithead son. He put his hands up to block its attack, and as Donna Fargo belted out the chorus of her biggest hit, Addie Jorgensen's hand snapped backward, his wrist breaking through the bone, his artery spraying his sister in the face, sending her into clotted wails of horror as blood pooled down her tiny face and into her mouth.

"There once was a time that I could not imagine how it would feel to say," Donna Fargo rang out as Mr. Jorgensen snapped out of shock and realized what was happening.

He shoved his chair back, it tipped from the sudden momentum, his body reeling backward, the base of his skull cracking on the chair behind his own. He fell motionless instantly to the floor. Addie Jorgensen leapt up, ran toward the back, slipped on a fresh jet of blood his wrist ejected, and smashed his face on the floor, a pool of blood flooding the black tile he landed on. He tried to push himself up and felt his hand break even more as he heard that woman, *that Affe* who couldn't just accept her place in the White World, step over him on either side.

He felt her sit on his back.

He felt her pull his head up by the back of his hair.

He watched as the floor came closer and further away, over and over as she smashed it into the floor.

Addie Jorgensen watched as his White World first turned Blood Red and then Pitch Black forever.

Rainbow smashed the boy's skull into the floor in a blind and primal rage until she heard a crying baby in the dining room. She looked at the little girl soaked in her dead brother's blood, her parents also dead on either side of her, and *Rainbow Connection* being sung by Karen Carpenter.

"Come on, let's get you cleaned up," Rainbow said.

"Ooh ooh, ooh, Affe!" Baby Jorgensen replied.

Rainbow carried the little girl to the prep table, careful not to slip and eat shit in any of Brother Addie's blood.

She laid the little girl on her back and remembered something Daddy told her when she first started cleaning chickens. "They got to be calm and peaceful, otherwise they'll never trust you enough to cleave their head off."

"Rainbows are visions, but only illusions and rainbows have nothing to hide.." Rainbow and Karen Carpenter sang to the baby as she stopped fussing.

"Would you kill baby Hitler?" Rainbow cooed at the girl.

"Ooh! Ooh! Ooh! Affe!" she blabbered back.

"Well, as long as we're on the same page," Rainbow said and brought the cleaver down on the girl's neck.

She closed her eyes and breathed rapidly, trying to think of a way to do this without getting caught, without throwing up, and most of all without ending up unaccounted for like the third man had when she was 20.
Or like whoever the recipes in the box and teeth in the wall belonged to.

If Rainbow had survived all of that so young before she knew anything, she could survive this. She didn't think of the blond bastards next door as people. And these four, the Jorgensen's, had said they were going to a 'pick-a-nick' tonight next door.
Is that what had happened to Didi?
Like Granddaddy had told her it would when she was little?
Like it had for Emmett Till the summer she turned ten.
If so, Rainbow decided she didn't give a flying rat's ass about one of them being a toddler.

In fact, one could argue the mouth portion of the headless baby, wherever it had rolled to, was the instigator of the entire thing. Everyone else had just cheered her on while she looked at Rainbow in one eye, Judith in the other, and quite literally aped at her.

She went to the steel sink and washed as much blood off her hands, cuticles and nails as possible. She went to double check the door and shades. She turned the lights down low and the music up loud and got to work cleaning the strangest meat delivery she had ever received.

She thought about the index cards and figured she would be able to get three full trays of perfectly smoked meat out of it and one "rotisserie chicken".

At 6:06pm, Judith "Rainbow" Jefferson began her meal prep work, breaking it down, sectioning cuts together, beating odd bits with the mallet and tossing them into an orange Home Depot bucket.

The bucket, along with however many trash bags it took for the Jorgensen remnants to fill and Rainbow would take a trip to the basement after the work up here was done. Make sausages with the bucket meat and dump the rest in the basement incinerator Granddaddy had installed in the summer of 1921. She worked all night, her CD player moving through all eight discs before clicking off without Rainbow noticing.
These cuts of pork and beef needed to look exactly right.

Chapter Seventeen

9/9/2008: The Way to a Man's Heart

"Soylent Green is people!"
~Charlton Heston

At 10:30 AM Rainbow heard knocking on the front door, certain it was police coming to investigate why the Jorgensen Klan hadn't shown up for their meeting last night. She could picture it now; a White cop holding up 4 hoods. Three large, one tiny.

"Ma'am, we can't locate the people these belong to. The little one was supposed to light the cross, that's how we knew something was wrong."

"Hello? Rainbow? Are you in there?" It was that boy, David. She had told him to come on the 9th of last month and again on the 9th of this month but in the excitement of everything last night she had completely forgotten he was coming today.

She cracked open the front door and said, "Hi, David. Today is actually no good. Meet me on the 72nd downtown 1/2/3 platform tomorrow morning at 10:45." She shut the door. "Wait!" She yelled at the door she herself had opened and shut. She pulled it open and said, "come back at 3:30 today. Food for the people next door. You can't eat any." She reclosed the door and bolted it before David could speak.

While David stood outside the door flabbergasted, Rainbow went back to the basement to finish grinding the final chunks of meat into the sausage casings. She had thrown two racks of *Adam's Ribs* into the smoker a little before 7:00 AM and could already smell the meat downstairs.
The index cards had been clear, the smell of the meat would draw everyone from blocks away.

By lunch people were knocking on the door every 5 minutes.
By 1:00 the phone was ringing asking what Rainbow was
smoking.

"Private order for a client. It's pork, you wouldn't want
any. You know how funny pork can be," she'd tell someone,
"oh, I found one of my granddaddy's old recipes and had to try
it for myself," she would tell another.
In between temp checks and reloading wood and crutching
one of the male Jorgensen's rumps in butcher paper because
the water content in it had stalled the meat, Rainbow went
through every possible response Gunnar would or could have
to what she said was about to try.
The trick to at the very least getting in the door was being
solved by David, and he was innocent as far as all of this was
concerned.

He was merely a Trojan horse, stuffed with soldiers,
Rainbow thought and started to laugh.

At 13:45 Gunter and Lukas were in the backyard of the Dog
Whistle and arguing about how to get rid of a motorized
wheelchair that sat half burned in the ashes and rubble of last
night's picnic and cross burning.

"We can throw it in the river," Lukas said.

"We can just take it up to the woods in the park,"
Gunter said, completely unaware Hino was behind him.

"And how would a woman in an electric chair get into
the river or up the hills and stairs of the park?" Hino booted
Gunter in the ribs. "No. Dig. Eight feet down. Over by the

back wall. Put the chair and anything from last night in it, pour in a bucket of maggots and cover it up."

At 3:30 PM exactly Rainbow heard three rapid taps on her front door. It was so right on time that for a moment she was nervous someone had found out about what the meat actually was.

"Rainbow? Rainbow please open up?" David was trying to stay calm as he saw Evangeline get out of her Benz and cross into the Dog Whistle. He hadn't seen her in person last night, not even her Falu lips in their usual place like during the meetings in Chicago, or Tulsa the one time she almost caught him there. But this was bad because it was broad daylight and he was in his Doc Martens with horizontal White Laces and in front of the 'Black Barbecue Bitch's' restaurant knocking.

If Gunnar came out to meet Evangeline both David and Rainbow would end up like the woman everyone but David had taken a stab at last night.
She was a woman David had seen a few times in the neighborhood.
It wasn't enough that Didi hadn't been one of the worst parts of the journey toward justice; it was that the woman last night had been in a motorized wheelchair.

**

Her legs were intact but immobilized from what David had gathered before hyperventilating in the bathroom for 10 minutes while he waited for the noise in the yard to die down. Her chair had run out of battery right outside the bar. Those two dipshits Gunter and Lukas, had pushed the chair into the bar and promised to plug it in just as soon as they showed her something. Lukas had bragged that as they pushed her into the meeting hall and she saw the red and black swastika flag she began to thrash and yell for help. She apparently had a small dog that she tossed to the floor and told to find help.

The dog ran to the door and began yapping and scratching until Lukas picked it up by the leash like a noose and carried it behind the bar.

Gunter bragged about what happened next as David watched Klansman after Klansman dig forks into the woman's leg asking if she could feel it.

Gunter had started saying that Lukas had raised the lid of the blender and dog high above his head and asked the woman which order they should go back in the blender.

That was when David said, "sorry, I want to know how high the speed on the blender was, but I have to piss. Four Pils' before Klanishness, that's on me."

**

Mercifully, Rainbow pulled the door open. David almost leapt inside.

"If being punctual is part of racist shitheadery, no wonder the trains in Germany ran on time," Rainbow said, pointing at David's shoes.

"It's hard getting in here without them noticing. It's even harder when the door is locked. What was so time sensitive but couldn't be handled at 10:30 this morning?"

"I need you to help me take this meat next door. And to make sure they take at least a bite," Rainbow saw hesitation and incredulity in David's eyes and said, "if I don't get customers soon I'll lose this place.

"What color are my eyes?" David asked.

"What? Blue...a really pretty blue, like ice water."

"I'm sorry, I can't help, not today. I promise to explain eventually, but I can't today. As it is, I saw her going into the bar so I shouldn't be willing to risk it, but if my eyes are blue today, I really can't," David saw the confusion in her face and decided not to tell her anything more in case her asking him to come at 3:30 and Evangeline's simultaneous arrival next door were related.

Suddenly David felt like this wasn't a restaurant, this was a trap. This was the place he had been lured to. If the last head of the Hydra was next door, this felt like the mouth.

"Was he with her? I guess I could take them each a plate," Rainbow trailed off in thought as an idea occurred to David.

"Go invite them here to talk. Tell them you have a proposition. A lot of the people at these meetings don't know what they're really getting into. If they met you just before they went there, maybe something would change. But what you tell him is you need money and cust—no. Tell him you miss serving people and that this place was WTO after your incident here in the sixties to keep the peace and stay afloat. That you'll give him $4 of each rib order and 40% of anything else. He'll probably tell you $5 on the ribs and 60% on everything else if he says yes. Make him eat a rib on it. These guys commit to their dipshit manly bit. To quote Gunnar, 'some things just are what they are.' A lot of these guys are dweebs and motards who didn't have a vent so this is what happens to them. They meet guys like them and pick the dumbest thing to be proud of and turn hate into activities. Also, I'm sorry, can I have a rib? They smell amazing." David finally stopped rambling as a defense mechanism.

"No. No you cannot have any of this. This is a peace offering and a plea for an ounce of humanity," Rainbow thought about how this meat was several ounces of humanity and stifled a laugh, David misread it as the first signs of crying and exhaled heavily.

"Believe me on a deep and human level when I tell you that next door and everyone inside of it is completely devoid of humanity. But money? Money talks. And knowing your place goes the full distance with all of them, as disgusting as it is," David's face was placid and his eyes were like daggers.

"Should I tie my hair in a kerchief and say 'yowza'?" Rainbow rolled her eyes at David.

"No, but you should wear gloves and tell them the meat is 100% American and organic, low fat, high protein, they're body obsessed if you haven't noticed."

"Hard to tell under the robes," Rainbow shot out.

"The, *what*?" David did his damnedest to play daft.

"You tell me to act like I know my place, in my actual place, but you don't have the decency to face facts and tell the truth. Like for instance why my bedroom window glows orange on every 8th of the month since they got here. I can't see the whole yard, but I can see it and his White Devil smile leering back up at me. His hoodless robe, glowing orange too," Rainbow stared David down.

David thought about Didi, and the woman from last night and however many others there had been here and at the rest of the Dog Whistles before they'd all been blown up and burnt down. He thought about how much danger both he and Rainbow were in until the final bar was brought down. "Can I see your bedroom window?"

"No." Rainbow thought about how the last three White men who had gone up her stairs had come back down dead, then she wondered if this icy blue eyed boy might hate Mondays as much as she did and led him up the back staircase.

As they climbed, she decided to be bold and asked the blunt questions, "how did you get involved with them? You seem so...not ignorant."

"Oh, thanks. I'd really rather not, but I will tell you, you're the closest thing to a friend I've made in a year and a half."

They walked into the upstairs apartment, Rainbow pausing to catch her breath. David couldn't believe how beautiful Rainbow's home was. Curios of brik-a-brak spanned the entirety of the second-half of the 20th century. Records and tapes, Polaroid photos and original playbills for Broadway shows in little stacks and piles.

"David, the last time a White man stood where you are, he died choking on molten hot lard. The man before him died with the cleaver in his neck at the bottom of those same stairs. A third man, according to legend, didn't exist. Or to others, turned into barbecue for killing my daddy with the tabletop RCA. But only I was here at the end of it all. That third man tried to kick my head in. He tried to rape me. He wound up peckerless and bleeding to death in my cellar in the dark. I was too scared the police would think what I did was heinous, but the truth is, I was a virgin then and I was until I was almost thirty. I didn't barbecue him. I sent his chopped up bits out with my regular Offal pickup and he probably ended up at a pig farm upstate and was digested into bacon fat. So I didn't cook and sell him, but someone probably did. So, again, how did you get involved with these people?"

"Gunnar yelled German into a phone while Evangeline murdered my mom in the background. Because three of his goons tried killing me but I gassed them in my bathroom. I've been to every one of their bars looking for him and a chance to get even ever since." David didn't flinch.

"And, no, the meat downstairs isn't human or spoiled, it really is a desperate attempt," Rainbow hoped it sounded honest and walked to the bedroom, pointing at the shut curtain.

David pulled it back just far enough to see that aside from where the cross might be visible, the area where the picnic took place was hidden behind the roof line.

He realized he'd been here too long.

Outside too long.

He wanted to run out the downstairs door and never say hello to Rainbow again so she could stay as uninvolved as possible.

David turned to Rainbow and said, "you said 10:30 on the downtown platform tomorrow?"

Rainbow caught his drift and said, "yes, be inconspicuous, now get out of here, I need to put on vinyl gloves and know my place."

Chapter Eighteen

10/31/2008: Spooks, Spirits, and the Holy Ghost

"For sale: baby shoes, never worn."
~unknown

Rainbow took a plate to the bar and waited while she heard men's voices yelling about who should open the door and who should or could be coming by unannounced in the middle of the day. Ultimately, a weird looking boy covered in dirt had answered, reeled back at the sight of a Black woman, but had promised to tell Gunnar she had come by.

Two hours later he returned with an empty plate, a little irritated, and said, "Was good. Did you wear gloves?"

That had been a little over six weeks ago.
Customers, not a lot regularly, but a lot on the 8th of this month, all White.
Gunnar had countered with what David told her.

A foot in the devil's door is one step closer to burning down Hell. But tonight was Halloween. A few kids had come in early to trick or treat, but then dozens of White Families came around 6 and cleared the kitchen by 8. She had sold almost $1000 worth of meat, but would only get around $400 once Gunnar got his cut. As Rainbow finished resetting the dining room, a man came in.

It was David, but his eyes were green. "Lock up, turn off the lights, call people and tell them to do the same."

David turned to leave just as quickly, bumping into two White men on the sidewalk outside, "fucking Coon didn't make enough meat!"
Rainbow heard him yell to the men.
She watched the three of them go toward the bar as she began to seethe.

First he told her to be safe and stay in, then he called her a coon loud enough for anyone on the street to hear.

Rainbow would be safe, but for Angelo Davis Junior, or as WNYC would call him for the next five days after tonight, 'Baby Angelo', Halloween 2008 would be his third and final and it would be all trick, no treat. He would die surrounded by ghosts.

At #45 there were people dressed in Klan robes, but there were also strange costumes. Mumming plays about White Knights killing Black Knights and two people dancing on a big piece of cardboard, soft shoeing on salt and Black face yelling "Boo!" at children from the neighborhood. Black Princesses and Spidermen carried pillowcases and plastic shopping bags.

And outside the MLK projects on 115th and Madison Avenue a little boy was last seen riding his electric four wheeler up and down the block in large lazy loops. He had turned 3 in September and gotten his four wheeler from his Pop-Pop.

At 7:28 PM, Lukas asked Baby Angelo if he could show him where the Subway was.

Angelo had driven to the far end of the sidewalk, past where his Mama told him he could go, and at a little before 7:00 AM tomorrow morning, his four wheeler will be found tossed inside a dumpster.

As Harlemites wait on line to vote on Tuesday morning, they'll
hear White voices murmuring about a *Martinmas Goose* they
picked apart on Halloween night.
How scary it would be if John McCain didn't win.
How many more little geese would end up picked apart?

But on Halloween night, as Lukas held Angelo under his
hoodie as he ran the half block to the Dog Whistle and
prepared to offer a Schwartzes Affe that would definitely earn
him a pair of Red Laces, all Baby Angelo wanted was his
Pop-Pop.

As they tied his tiny body to the cross and lit matches,
Rainbow thought she heard a baby wail in the distance for just
a moment as Gunnar handed Lukas a new pair of Blood Red
Laces.

David's body went on autopilot and he pretended all these
ghosts were only roasting a chicken.

The moment he got home, he threw up everything in his
stomach and collapsed onto his bed, sobbing himself to sleep.

FOURTH INTERLUDE

11/4/2008: Hope & Change

"Yes We can!"
~President Obama

In the late hours of November 4th, 2008, Hope and Change arrived in America.

At Grant Park in Chicago, Barack Hussein Obama was elected 43rd President of the USA. He spoke to a crowd of almost a quarter million people and countless more, both nationally and around the world. Almost 2/3 of the eligible voting population came to the polls and cast ballots for America's first unique president since Kennedy. Throughout his speech he quoted Kennedy, Lincoln, Dr. King, and events in the course of human history as momentous as this. Once quoting the marches from Selma to Montgomery, saying, "the arc of the moral universe is long, but it bends toward justice."

Most heroic of all President Obama's phrases that warm November night was, "If there is anyone out there who still doubts that America is a place where all things are possible, who still wonders if the dream of our Founders is alive in our time, who still questions the power of our democracy to night, is your answer."

Chapter Nineteen

11/8/2008: Declaration Day

*"Whosoever slayeth Cain,
vengeance shall be taken on him sevenfold."*
~Henry Wadsworth Longfellow

"We should have done more sooner."

A waiter set a pork chop in front of Rainbow and a wedge salad in front of Lisa and a crock of French onion soup in front of David. The waiter disappeared and the three of them stared at one another, trying to figure out who had said it.

And if it hadn't been Rainbow clearing her throat and saying, "no, something this terrible isn't about playing the long game. It's not even about casualties of war. This. This is exactly what I was afraid of the day I met them. The 28th is handling this like they did when I was a little girl to a boy called James Powell. They kept saying they're doing their best, but I know that I and at least fifty other people have called and told them to knock on #45's door but they won't. But they already know and have seen all the new White faces in the neighborhood and don't want to scare them."

David looked at both women and said, "Rainbow, you're right, you've been right this whole time. I've chased those two across five States and permanently shut down every bar but this one. And what happens at those meetings is far worse than the burning cross they make you look at. Today is eight days that he's been missing, which means it's been seven since he died back there." David realized both Lisa and Rainbow had stopped eating. "I apologize, I just, after all of it, from Harlem to Chicago, all of it feels like something inevitable. This is the only place I've met someone like you, Rainbow, and you do deserve the actual truth. Learning that you both have been fighting this for over a year before I even got here, learning about how careful you are to only meet here, only on a verbal schedule. And I'm so used to it all that I moved basically next door and thought they would never notice me.

Lisa looked at David and said, "oh, if you think she's been patient, I have to hide 12 duffel bags and pretend I'm flat broke. Rainbow owns her house. I have to invent reasons why my rent is late. Plus, did you know that nobody in the world has ever thought carrying bag after bag of chlorine tablets into a fifth floor walk up on 136th is normal? But once a month I leave here, go up to the Home Depot on 23rd and watch the clerks look at me cross eyed. Take them on the Uptown 2 and hope I don't see two people I couldn't pick out of a lineup. Or worse, my ex, who I'm certain is part of the cabal. So, no, it wasn't that, what you said. It was the fact that you are a *baby*. What are you, 22?" Lisa looked at Rainbow.

"Life doesn't wait until 40 to hit you in the head, Lisa. Baby Angelo, and yes, David, are proof of that. I for one am glad to know that this may be my fight, but this is his, and yours too.

"Lisa, Rainbow, the truth is that I think you both should abandon your plan and do what the Steve Miller Band suggested," David winked at Rainbow. "Lisa, I might be 20, but I learned the hard facts first. So if this is what I have to do now, I can rest at 21 and be done."

They all laughed.

"No." Rainbow said, "We keep our plan, you keep yours, if we're lucky, they'll both succeed and we can all be 21 and done together."

**

"Freunde, der große Affe unsere Wahl gestohlen! Even after we took one of their young just before the day! You all saw the lines, you saw how the Affen jumped for joy to vote for hope and change. You saw them ignore our warnings about what would happen if they decided to go Planet of the Apes on us. 14 words. Say them with me, brothers and sisters, if now isn't the time to believe in the God-given power of our Whiteness, when is? Say it with me. We must secure the existence of our people and a future for White children. Again. We must secure the existence of our people," Gunnar Erichsen raised his arm to 45 degrees and finished, "and a future for White children. Tonight matters. The coming weeks matter. If we can gain full control of Haarlem and restore the soil to Dutch blood, maybe the rest of the country will rise up too."

The room erupted in chants of, "RAHOWA! RAHOWA!"

Gunnar raised both hands to quiet the room. "Before we go, please know that I mean those final seven words deeply. Evangeline, *my wife*, is pregnant."

Chapter Twenty

12/19/2008: Kindling Wood

"Is that all there is?"
~Peggy Lee

Rainbow woke up early that Friday morning prepared to bring her own long national nightmare to an end. She laid on her bed and looked up through her bedroom window for what would be the last time, the sky gray with wisps of clouds swimming quickly along a breeze.

Lisa woke up at 5:45, remembered what today was, and hit snooze, twice. She had never even hit someone, let alone gassed a whole apartment building full of people. And unlike Rainbow's part of the execution, she wouldn't know if it worked or not until she saw it on the news or on Yahoo! in a few days when none of the tenants made it home for Christmas.

David's alarm went off at 6:00.
He'd slept for exactly 20 minutes.
He got out of bed and did his reps of 87s, then turned the shower to cold and got in.
        "Today is the end," David said to himself, "sieg für die Blauäugige Ratte," and turned the water to full hot and enjoyed his first hot shower in 2 1/2 years.

On 136th Street Gunnar held his sister's belly while they talked about the agenda for the final prep meeting before the night of reckoning planned for the 25th.
Or as that probate who brought them to the toddler at Sint Maarten's Nacht had started calling it "KKKwanzaa."

"When do you think I'll feel our son kick," he asked.

"Not for another month, but he hears your voice and knows you're going to build him the Whitopia Mutter and Vater dreamt of," Evangeline pulled Gunnar's hand tighter around her waist and purred. Outside their door she heard dozens of boots marching down the hall and stairs in unison.

The sun rose across Harlem like it had every morning since before Harlem was Haarlem and before that; but today, the sun felt different.
Like it was about to shine a beam on every dark thing, and let winter freeze it to death.

Chapter Twenty-One

12/08/2008: All Fir One, One Fir All

"Pack up all my cares and woe, here I go,
winging low, bye, bye, blackbird."
~Miles Davis

At 10:30 AM a semi truck parked outside Rainbow's Joint and began unloading 600 Balsam Firs.

At 11:45 AM when he finished, Rainbow handed him a plastic bag with four takeout containers full of $5000 each and a separate container loaded with the best and last barbecue she would ever cook.
The kitchen was closed, and once Christmas came and went, so would she.

At 11:59 when Gunnar turned on 116th street he saw a chain link fence at the far end of the block and then noticed the stacks of fence panels leaning on the wall outside his passenger window.

He parked, walked past #45 and asked Rainbow, "what the fuck is this?"

"This," Rainbow told him, "was the last Christmas in Harlem."

"You're selling?" Gunnar asked.

"No, foreclosure. It'll go up for auction in the spring. Rough final year and a half for the economy. Maybe you're right. Maybe a change is coming."

"So you're going to sell trees until the end of the month? And then, just, what? Go? You're from here, Where would you even go?"

Rainbow squared her eyes on Gunnar's, "Well, maybe somewhere out West, like Seattle or maybe Portland..."

"Well, this is too many trees, It was a waste of money.
How much is the mortgage? Maybe I could buy it and let you
live out your days making barbecue in servitude…"

"There's the racist piece of shit I met last April, maybe
I'll sell all of these, maybe I won't. Maybe I'll sell the other
eight-hundred and eighty-eight I have coming between now
and the 25th. Maybe I'll make enough to save my home and
watch you burn in Hell from my bedroom window."

"I'm glad you've seen me back there, Rainbow. What
kind of Grand Dragon would I be if I couldn't even scare a
little old Negress?"

This time it was Rainbow who cleared her throat and sent a
cold December loogie all over Gunnar's dumb mustache.
Rainbow raised her hand to 45 degrees, silently turned and let
her arm fall, and walked inside.

Gunnar stood silent, flabbergasted and seething. Steam
pillowed in the noon air from his booger covered mustache and
the bells of Saint John the Divine rang out.

**

At the meeting that night, Gunnar told his Klan that there
would be no picnic or cross burning. Instead they would wait
until the upstairs lights in that Black Barbecue Bitch's house
went out and then they'd break branches off the trees out front
and make as many unsalable as possible.

At 8:25 PM David walked out of the Dog Whistle and turned toward Morningside.

He said he forgot his smokes at home and needed to buy a pack.

"It's easier than bumming one over and over," he had said. He rapped twice on the dining room window and kept going.

He came back 15 minutes later with a carton of Marlboro Reds, rapping twice again on Rainbow's window on his way to the bar and passed them out while saying, "Now we can wait all night if we need."

On cue, Rainbow turned her lights off and then went to the balcony and silently watched as the monsters next door did exactly what they had hoped they would.

Like cavemen gathering wood for a fire that hadn't been invented yet, she saw them rend branches and toss them into the street. She watched as one, then two, then five men pissed on them. She smiled as Gunnar broke the tops off dozens of the Firs.

"Good," she whispered to herself, "show off your strength. It won't do you a damned bit of good in the end, but you're making light work of my load now."

She went inside and slept deeply, the sound of crackling wood playing in her ears, images of wheelbarrows filled with debris dancing in her head.

Chapter Twenty-Two

12/19/2008: The Mice in Council

"My friends, it takes a young mouse
to think of a plan so ingenious and yet so simple.
With a bell about the cat's neck to warn us we shall all be safe.
I have but one brief question to put to the supporters of the plan—
which one of you is going to bell the cat?"
Moral: it is one thing to propose, another to execute.
~Aesop

"Even if you are not ready for the day,
it cannot always be night."
~Gwendolyn Brooks

At 10:30 AM, the Christmas Tree truck pulled onto 116th Street for one last delivery of 444 assorted Firs. Ordering 1,488 trees with only three months' warning had been difficult, but cash is king and it had only taken 1/5 of a single duffel bag to get this many after the vandalism on the 8th.
444 trees arrived on Friday the 12th, and now these.

"If 1500 matchsticks doesn't do it, I don't know what will," Rainbow said to the sky.

Christmas trees filled the sidewalk.
They filled the curbside and redirected traffic with their pinecones, branches striking the sides of cars, cabs, and MTA buses.

Every night, some of those little peckerwoods would snap branches and chuck pinecones at the dining room window.

During the day they would spit on the window and yell "PERCHTA AFFE".

They came and went from the Dog Whistle at all hours now..

She would start to rub the meat mallet and staple gun in her apron pocket and then think, *there's not enough spit and piss in all of you to handle your night tonight*, and go back to remembering the plan.

For what to do if Lisa didn't knock on the glass at 7:05pm sharp.

How she didn't come this far in the arc of her life's journey to need any help beyond the woman inside her to get anything done and defeat any Goliath.

At 10:45 AM, Judith's internal grasp on things and Rainbow's cool exterior almost shook.
Gunnar Erichsen had pulled up.
Rainbow could see red lips in the passenger seat.
But when the back door opened and Matthew got out, she almost threw up.

He made his way across the street and into the maze of trees.
He was coming over to talk to her.
Rainbow felt her hand pull the staple gun handle tight.
		"Merry Christmas, Rainbow. What are all of these???"
Matthew's false and even smile gleamed in the low winter sun.
		"A paper mill. What does it look like?"
		"Not a restaurant, which is what you're licensed as. This is disruptive to traffic and an illegal operation. How many of these do you even have? They look like someone tore half of the branches off."
		"One Thousand, Four-Hundred and Eighty-Eight. If I sell them all for at least $50, it'll cover what I'm behind. If I don't, I'll have enough wood to build a hut in the woods with. Why? You want to buy one? or eight? *You* did this, Matthew. You took a bag of money almost two years ago. From *those* people. And now I'm losing a restaurant and home that's been in my family since my granddaddy Freeman built the upper

level himself. All ripped away by racist shitbags and a broken, desperate divorcee in the same year a Black Man became President. Slavery ended, but nothing changed. Is there anything else? Want me to spit in your face the way your leader did to me in front of everyone at the opera? Want to call me a nigger just once to my face? Why did you come now?"

 Matthew stared, slack jawed, unable to say anything. Rainbow was right.
The Erichsens had swooped in and declared Harlem belonged to them because the Dutch had settled it half a millennia ago.
 This was a little old lady who was terrorized by her neighbors in the third leg of her life.
This was a woman who had survived a night that her father had not.
Matthew saw beyond the Rainbow.
He saw a warrior inside, honing her sword on the wood of a Fir tree.
Matthew backed away silently.

At just after 11 AM, Lisa opened the door to the roof of the apartment she had paid cash for, sight unseen, as long as the landlord gave her a key to the roof.
        "Don't make me pay almost two grand a month to climb almost to heaven and not let me go up and look once in a while," she had said, and then patted his arm, but now it seemed crazy.

She needed to extend a telescopic ladder across the small but very real gap between this roof and the three connected roofs of her old Mediterranean Avenue properties.

She then had to carry four Timbuktu backpacks up to the water tower, dump in more chlorine than a YMCA keeps on hand, get into the building, light a fire inside the building, get out of the building, climb back across the ladder, and then catch the first train after 7:30 PM to 116th Street, run two blocks without seeing Matthew, and then hope Rainbow and David finished the end of the collective plan.

"Simple enough," Lisa said to herself as she sat down a pair of bags and then began pulling rung after rung from the ladder and prayed to God it was long enough as she let it swing down like a felled tree, the hard plastic caps of the top clanging against the bricks at the edge evenly.

Lisa got to work. She figured it would take at least an hour to empty each backpack filled with chlorine into the water tower, At least four hours to fully mix, and then a 10 minute window to get inside, start a fire big enough to set off every sprinkler inside of the buildings, get out before it happened, and then the rest.

At 12:37, Lisa dumped the last bag of chlorine tabs into the water tower and climbed down. She tested the door to the roof, hoping that not only would it open, but not screech in alarm. When she did, the latch clicked, and aside from a low creak, opened without issue.

Lisa closed the door gently and crossed the extended ladder
back to her secret next door apartment and checked her final
fifth backpack.
Eight cans of Sterno glinted in the light from above.
She checked the front pouch for two lighters and three books
of matches, closed it and rested in the corner, set her watch
alarm for 4:00 PM and tried to rest.

Over the last three months, David had managed to embed
himself perfectly into the Haarlem Dog Whistle, and had done
it the way that was always most natural to him in any situation,
by being helpful.
At first he'd offered to clean up the meeting hall, then he would
take the trash out, and after the meeting on the 8th, he'd gone
up the block to buy a carton of Marlboro Reds for everyone to
share in the backyard at 8:30 after the rally but before the
picnic.
The meeting on the 12th had ended with Gunnar saying he
needed volunteers with a special project on the 19th. David had
been third to volunteer.

He had left his apartment at 7:30 AM, taking the B to Penn
Station, walked to the 1, gone down to Park Place, walked past
St. Paul's Chapel and to the 9/11 Memorial. He had sat on a
bench and watched the Hudson River lap and rush out to sea.
He thought about how every drop of water in the river had
come from the base of Mount Marcy in the Adirondacks, from
a place called Lake Tear of the Clouds. Sure, rain and snow

added to the rushing waters, but every drop made it to the sea just the same. He remembered being a little boy, shuttling 1,000 miles twice a summer and every other Christmas between two houses that didn't want him. During the school year he was bullied relentlessly for not being like other boys during the day. On nights and weekends, his stepdad beat him mercilessly, and by the time he was nine, he'd begun making him give him hand and blowjobs while he watched NASCAR and David's mom went grocery shopping.

David thought about how he'd gone to his dad's full time for two years until the day he came out, how a man named Charlie had given him a ride to Chicago and said no when David asked if Charlie wanted head.
He thought about how he had met Val, and for a brief window in his life at the end of his youth, he'd had a mother before Gunnar's Voice and Evangeline's gun ripped her away.
He thought about how his real parents hadn't even sent a friend request to his pictureless Facebook profile in the five years he'd had it.
He thought about the people Gunnar and all his Dog Whistlers must have terrorized before he'd found them.
How many *picnics* they must have had, how many Baby Angelos had gone missing across America since whenever these bars had started popping up in minority neighborhoods. For a while, he considered whether what he had done was, and was about to do for the final time, terrorism, whether it was as bad to put down bad dogs as it was to put down sick ones. If putting these Dog Whistlers down was terrorism in the way

hijacking planes and crashing two of them into the Twin Towers had been. Was what they had been doing in five states worth what he, Rainbow and Lisa were going to do to them?

"Would you kill baby Hitler?" David said to himself as he stood up and walked to the Uptown 2 and popped his green contacts in.

The 2 train pulled into the 116th St. station and David gasped audibly as he saw giant red swastikas and graffiti reading, "The Freedom Party FUCK the Democrats!" David stepped off the train and saw Gunter and Lukas coming up from the far end of the platform, hands splattered with paint.

"Heil, Max!" they both yelled as they raised their arms at him. For a moment, he forgot they knew his face and name. He cleared his throat and raised his own arm.

"Heil, Gunter. Heil, Lukas. Wunderschöne Graffiti." The three of them walked up to the street, pausing at the top of the stairs so Gunter could draw Stars of David on the entrances to the subway. As they crossed Lenox, David saw Gunnar handing Rainbow a wad of money. Gunnar turned just in time to see the obvious look of confusion on all three boy's faces.

"Heil Soldaten!" Gunnar barked and raised his arm.

"Heil Kommandant!" all three yelped back, arms at 45 degrees, David avoiding Rainbow's gaze at all costs.

"I just bought 100 of these trees to take to unfortunate people in the neighborhood. Could you boys begin loading as many into the backyard as you can? Someone has been vandalizing these out here at night so it'll be safer in the back." Gunnar's voice was playful but clear as they each grabbed an end of a Fir. Gunter and Lukas on one, Gunnar and 'Max' on the other. The door to Number 45 opened and into the sunlight emerged those unmistakable Falu Red lips.

"You can carry them, I'll hold the door," she said, smiling.
Gunter and Lukas went first.

As Gunnar passed Evangeline he said, "this is Max," and she had said hello while staring at his eyes.

Once they were inside, Gunnar told Max, "each of these will go to the house of an Affe, a bomb strapped to the inside, all set for the 25th. At Zero Hundred hours, they'll all go in their sleep. We'll make up to a Merry Christmas indeed."

And that was the moment David stopped thinking of any Dog Whistler as anything but a mutt.

It took the four of them two hours and twenty minutes to move 50 trees to the Biergarten. They had to stop from 1:40 to 2:00 to sleep on the floor. Evangeline had insisted. It took another 45 minutes to move 50 in front of the window and anchor three pieces of temporary chain link fence around it. Both Rainbow and Max had avoided looking at one another for fear of laughing at how Gunnar was helping them without knowing.

At 3:30, Gunnar asked Max if he wanted to go to the dorms on 136 with Gunter and Lukas to nap before tonight. He declined, saying he had to get downtown to feed his cat. That was when Evangeline's ears perked up.

"What kind of cat? I have a Maine Coon named Pistenraupe."

"Rattenfanger," David said.

"Well if you want to come to 136th you could meet Pistenraupe...if you want."

"No, I really shouldn't."

"I'm driving the boys anyway, You can catch the train from there."

As Evangeline parked on 136th and got out, David's heart sank. Gunnar had stayed behind to finish organizing for tonight. Gunter and Lukas had gone wordlessly inside when they arrived. She had asked Max to wait here with her for a moment.

"These boys believe in the cause, but need teammates to win. You're a lone wolf. Don't get too close to any of them. They're all followers."

She walked him to the fifth floor and toward the rooftop door. David felt sick. She stopped one apartment door before then and he felt even worse.

She showed him a Luger, "it was my Vater's." She offered him a glass of water. He asked for a Pilsner. When she went into the bathroom, David was convinced she'd either come out naked or aiming a gun at him. He was right about one, nude.

"Gunnar knows," she said when she reemerged. "He loves knowing other men enjoy me. If you've ever used the glory hole at the bar, I'm the mouth on the other side. But you were so helpful today that I thought I'd thank you properly."

She pulled her vagina open with her fingers and David cleared his throat.

"Could I use the restroom?"

"Oh, I suppose you did work up a sweat. You saw where the bathroom is."

David went in and closed the door. That was when he heard something in the shower growl and hiss. David pulled back the curtain and saw a kennel in the tub. At the back was a pure white cat the size of a Rottweiler leering at David. He bit his tongue and went pee. He washed his hands and when he came back out, Evangeline was laying on the bed, touching herself.

"Why is there a cat in the tub?"

"Oh, that's my Pistenraupe. But he's better for home defense if we don't socialize him."

She took his hand and guided it down the gentle curve of her small baby bump and against the warm, soft mound of her vulva. On the scale of disgusting things David had done in his life, he decided this was one of the worst. As Evangeline pressed his middle and index fingers into her vagina, he felt himself turn into the little boy he'd once been when Frank had made him "pull on it gently" as the race cars on TV made an endless series of left turns. Evangeline's phone chimed.

"Birth control alarm, every day at 1645, I never turned it off," she said while she caressed her belly and looked up at Max.

As she rocked her pelvis faster and faster, David felt a wave of sorrow and disgust wash over himself, and he began to cry.

"Was ist los, Kleiner Wolf?" Evangeline asked.

"Ich bin eine Jungfrau," Max said in reply as a tear fell and splashed off her side.

"Oh, I just assumed you were a stud."

"Mein Fokus liegt auf der Ursache," another tear fell.

Internally, David was contemplating what killing a pregnant woman would mean to his conscience. His internal voice whispered, "*Baby Hitler*," and he moved his left hand to the top of the bed and grasped a pillow.
Evangeline reached up to caress *Max's* face and rubbed his left orbital bone with her right thumb. As she pulled her thumb across his lower lid, he felt a small pop in his eye and watched as a single green contact fell and landed on her breast.
She looked up at him. One green eye, one blue.
"DIE BLAUÄUGIGE RATTE!"

David yanked the pillow and held it over her face. Evangeline kicked and scratched and clawed at the blue eyed rat. She tried to yell, but it hit the pillow with muffled groans.
David held the sides of the pillow down as hard as he could. Fingernails dug out chunks of flesh on his arms, knees and elbows bashed against him, but he held firm.

As she reached the end of the oxygen in her lungs, she grabbed the edge of the mattress and pulled herself toward the foot of the bed as hard as she could. David watched as Evangeline's chin appeared, then her mouth, nose, and eyes, all in a half second. She ran full speed into the bathroom and slammed the door. She began to scream at the top of her lungs for help.

David went into the living room and grabbed the Luger.

That was when he heard the bathroom door open and then close again.

He heard the pattering of small feet and realized it must be the giant cat.
Lisa *had* managed to fall asleep. and when her watch beeped at 4:00 PM she leapt to her feet. She emptied the backpack and counted everything again. 8 sternos, 3 matchbooks, and 2 lighters. She pulled the lids off the Sterno cans and put them back in the bag. She put a matchbook in each pocket along with a lighter and returned the third to the front pocket of the backpack.

At 5:05, Lisa climbed across the ladder rungs and up the water tower in the last glow of sunset. She pulled the service door open and was met with what smelled like a hotel pool. She climbed back down and walked to the door she checked earlier. She could hear a woman screaming and what sounded like a caterwaul coming from an animal.

She checked her watch, 5:20.
She decided that even if she was caught, the fire would still take out everyone in the buildings and that dying wouldn't be in vain. Lisa pulled the door open and crept inside.

As she passed the first apartment door, she heard the noises again, coming from inside, and then a young man's voice yelling.

    "Both of you stay in there, I have the gun."

She knew it was David.
Lisa remembered how David had told them both to cut the bait and run after Baby Angelo.
She thought about Matthew and how this was all his fault.
Lisa pressed on.
When she reached the stairs she pulled a can of Sterno out and began scooping the gel out and rubbing it on the floor and walls. She took globs of it and flung them at sprinklers on the ceiling and prayed this would work, that her understanding of chemistry and building deterioration would hold up.

Lisa squatted down and began pulling the Sterno out of another can and making a trail of it down the hall toward the rooftop door. As she passed the apartment where the yelling was coming from, a young man came up the stairs and yelled.

"HALT!"
"There's someone screaming in there," Lisa pointed.
"That is the Erichsen's apartment," the boy said.
A fresh wave of screams came from behind the door.
The boy ran to it and knocked hard.

Max answered the door.
Half cracked, only his Right eye visible, still green.
"Heil, Hino. What's the problem?"
"This lady," Hino pointed at Lisa, "heard screaming."
David and Lisa locked eyes.
"Well, if you really want to know, Ev was thanking me for helping today at..." David stared at Hino.

"Oh! Haha! She's a real cat in the sack!"

"Yeah, I don't know how I'm going to handle this alone," David looked at Lisa again.

"Let me help," Hino said. "The trainees are all going to sleep for their evening 20 before tonight."
Hino pushed his way in, he walked to the bedroom and as he opened the door, Pistenraupe launched at his neck and knocked him to the ground.

Sprays of blood jetted across the white fur of the cat.
As Hino tried to grab the cat, its claws sliced his fingers and palms to ribbons.

David stood over them both and pulled the trigger.
First the head of the cat exploded, and then Hino's jaw did the same.

The bathroom door opened and Evangeline lunged at David with a nail file.

David didn't hesitate. He didn't have time for a grandiose speech about putting bad dogs down. He pulled the trigger and watched as a lotus of crimson bloomed across Evangeline's belly.

"I'd kill baby Hitler, and his mother too," he stared at Evangeline's Falu lips and pulled the trigger a third time.
The now half headless woman's body fell to the floor.

"We need to go!" Lisa yelled, deafened by the gunfire.

"Right, finish making the trails to the door. I need to grab one more thing."
David went into the bedroom and grabbed Evangeline's BlackBerry.
They each lit a book of matches and threw them against the Sterno slicked floor. A wave of blue fire ran down the hall and up the walls and just like that, they watched as small glass bulb after small glass bulb exploded, spraying gray water everywhere.

Then the smell of bleach hit them both and they watched as everything turned to a cloud of rust colored gas, they slammed the door.

In a small apartment downstairs, Gunter and Lukas heard screaming and gunfire for a moment before gray water erupted from the ceiling. They both ran for the apartment door, as Lukas grabbed the handle he felt his back, arms, and eyes and lungs begin to burn as the once gray cloud turned rust brown and coated their mouths with an acidic and tangy slick.

Blood erupted from Gunter's mouth.

Lukas opened the door and saw bodies spilling out of the neighboring units, rivers of blood and vomit running down the hallway. Lukas made it to the stairs before coughing up fresh clumps of lung tissue and falling over the banister, head splitting on the lobby floor below.

Lisa scampered across the ladder and David followed. They ran full speed down to the lobby before pausing by the mailboxes in the vestibule to catch their breath and see if anyone had made it outside. After 2 minutes had gone by and not a soul passed, they opened the door and went outside.
The windows next door were coated in brown, some streaked with the ghosts of handprints sliding downward. Small waterfalls of rusty air dripped out of a few lifeless panes.

They walked silently toward Lenox Boulevard.

When they reached the downtown station, they stared at graffiti on top of graffiti. Swastikas, SS Logos, 88s, HHs, and on top of it, in White spray paint, was the number **122514**.

"What do you think it means?" Lisa asked as they waited for the train to arrive in 3 minutes.

"It's a dog whistle. They speak in code because even though they're convinced everyone else is inferior, they don't have the guts to just say the hateful shit out loud. Like, 14 is a code for 14 words, a racist phrase about a White future that's 14 words long. Most of them can't quote it accurately, so they say '14 words.' As if that's not bad enough, they say '5 words,' which means to tell the cops 'I have nothing to say.' 88 means HH for Heil Hitler. 1488 is American Nazi code. You know about the laces, but there's a whole lot more. This graffiti is about a 'White Christmas.'"

David saw a bloodied and brown body struggle through the stile. He reached into his coat pocket and thumbed the Luger.

The body came shambling toward them, blood trickling from its mouth. It opened its jaw to speak, and a fresh gush of blood spewed out all over David's boots and Lisa's sneakers.
David wrapped his hand around the butt of the gun and yanked it from his pocket high above his head and brought it down on the unexplainable survivor's skull. He sat the body against the back side of the trash can and saw the light of the train at the end of the tunnel come closer and closer until the downtown 2 pulled into the station. The doors opened and as he and Lisa sat in the double seat at the end he realized he was covered in blood and rust.

"Oh, no! You can't show up like this! They'll know you were involved when nobody—" David squeezed Lisa's leg to shut her up.
He looked at the seven people in the car with them.
5 Black men, One Chinese woman, and an elderly Mexican man at the opposite end.

"You can't just say shit out loud, Lisa. What if someone, or a cop, had been in here?"

Lisa squeezed David's knee and smiling said, "5 words. I thought you'd learned their ways."
They both laughed.
The 125th stop came and went, 116th and 110th did too.
At 96th, they got off and walked up and over the passageway to catch an Uptown 2.
They got off at 110th and walked the back way.

As they passed the shady doorways between 115th and 116th, David thought of Didi and how she hadn't deserved to die in all of this.

"Before the corner, you go first and tell me if you see Gunnar. If you do, keep going Uptown. I need to get into my apartment and he might see me," David said.

"What? I thought we were going to Rainbow's?"

"We are, pit stop first. Turn Right if he's not there, keep going if he is."

Lisa turned Right.

David followed and then ran into the doorway of #53 ahead of her. He pulled three keys on a small ring out of his pocket and unlocked the main door.
He walked up the first flight of stairs, Lisa followed.
He walked up the second flight and Lisa felt woozy.
He jangled a square gold key between his fingertips as he rounded the corner.

Lisa felt like fainting as he slid the key into the deadbolt of number 7, and decided God had to have some Divine Plan that nobody else knew they were in on.

"Even though it's a crash pad, I try to feel like myself in my home. You're the only person besides a broker I never met that knows I'm the guy living in Apartment 7. Also, yes, I think those are shotgun pellet marks in my floor. I think someone was shot here before I moved in. I just thought I should say something after what you heard me do today, they're not my bullet holes, and welcome to my home."

David pushed the door open and Lisa didn't see a roach infested Crack Den with police crawling all over and photographing a body on the floor while a single fish swam in a dirty tank, unaware that it would soon also be dead but with zero fanfare.

"John Richards," Lisa said, slack-jawed.
The door to #7 at 53 West 116th swung shut and Lisa LeBlanc began to weep and heave as she ran her fingertips over the six tiny holes in the floor.

At 6:15 PM Evangeline's phone began to blare The Night They Drove Old Dixie Down and David stared as Gunnar's phone number paraded across the bottom of the screen for the second time in his life. David prepared to hear Gunnar's voice on the phone, and like the first time, he decided to remain voiceless and just listen.
"Ev? Nobody's here yet. None of the Triads who were supposed to help open these trees up. Ev? Ev?" Gunnar began to panic. He didn't have the car, he had no trained backup, and 50 trees fully branched out in the backyard with timers, C4, and spool after spool of wiring all over the place.
What if one of them had been a little too loose lipped to Matthew and he'd gone to the cops?

A woman screamed in the background and the line went dead. Gunnar fell to his knees, unsure whether to be grateful it wasn't the Feds busting him for domestic terrorism or to be afraid of whatever caused that scream.
He had heard his sister wail and scream since they were babies, but never like that.
There was a knock at the door.

Gunnar realized he was the only person in the bar and pulled himself together as he turned the lock and pushed the door open.

There stood Rainbow holding a plate of barbecue.

"I wanted to thank you for buying so many of my trees. I know I won't sell them all. But this money will help me start over, whatever that means at 64."

"Well, think of it as an investment in ridding this side of the street of any other owners. Come January, Matthew is selling us the apartments on the other side of you, so you'd just end up feeling like a monkey in the middle anyways," he grabbed the plate from her gloved hands.

"It's probably my fault for not letting you and your wife lay into me when we met, but here I am like a cowering dog offering thank you meat for your charity today. She tried looking into the bar, but his enormous build blotted it all out.

"Is that it?" Gunnar felt his pulse quicken when she mentioned Evangeline and wanted this conversation over.

"I have a little extra meat left that I cooked along with this if you want it, no charge. It's half a brisket and some rabbit and venison links. Cooking my Granny Caledonia's recipes until I don't have anywhere to make them anymore."

"I'll send someone to pick it up around 20:30, if you think it can wait, I'm busy."

"Sure, I'll be around."

The door closed before Gunnar could see a devious smile quietly creep across Rainbow's face. She walked back to the smoker and stared at the space where the fence slat had been before she pulled it down after Gunnar had opened three rows of trees against his side of the fence and beyond.

She swiped the dog collar hanging on the door to the smoker and read the name.

She pulled the door open and said, "smelling good, Mörder. Cooking right like some hot dogs should."

When the dog had come calmly, *curiously* through the hole and licked her hand, she debated not going through with it. Then remembered the horrible things Gunnar had done and all the loner, last tables of the night, first table of the afternoon, Neo-Nazis she'd slaughtered and dumped into the basement all Autumn long.

"Fuck it," Rainbow had said and brought Granddaddy Freeman's axe down hard and fast before the dog could even yelp.

She'd made ribs as best she could and turned the rest into links laced with every bottle of Lantus insulin she'd managed to get a prescription for over the summer when she switched doctors and told the new one she was insulin dependent since she was 57. The new doctor wanted to test her for Diabetes but Rainbow had told the *White Lady Doctor* that she knew what she was talking about and got the scripts.
She didn't care that some bottles were expired or whether or not it would actually work, only that she wanted to try anything on earth to exterminate the rabid dogs next door.

At 7:05, there was a triple tap pattern at her door.

Lisa's voice whispered, "Rainbow, hurry up.

"Girl, what is it?" Rainbow asked as she opened the door and saw that Lisa had been crying. "Lisa, honey, come on, sit down. What is it? Is it David? Did something go wrong? What?"

"John Richards," Lisa said as she sat down.

"What? The dead man from down the street? What, did walking by there remind you of better days and make you teary eyed?"

"David has been living in John Richard's old apartment since he moved here. He saw it listed on Craigslist at the beginning of July. Emailed Matthew without meeting and Western Unioned him 10 grand for a year long lease. He picked up the keys from the old bodega on the 3rd of July. He warned me about the bullet marks on the floor. I thought I was dead. I thought I was having a nightmare or was in hell or a coma. He's been up there in #7 this whole time without you or Gunnar or anyone seeing him there. How?!" She finished.

"Well, hard to look around when all you see are Nazis everywhere. Everyone has moved out, and he's more clever than anyone I've ever met. As far as it being that apartment? That's God putting that boy right where he needed to be. But Lisa, I'm here on earth wondering what the fuck happened on 136th.

Lisa remembered the rusty zombie and shuddered. She looked at Rainbow and began to cry again. "He was amazing. Calm and even. Like he'd been preparing for today since forever. He killed her, Rainbow. With their dad's gun. *Their*, Rainbow. They're *siblings*."

"But she was pregnant? *He killed a pregnant woman?*"

"With her brother's baby, Rainbow!"

Rainbow could and couldn't believe it.

Lisa continued, "The Sterno worked. The bulbs all burst from the water pressure change, and then," she held her arms against her chest, "then the gray water turned rust brown and we slammed the door. I could hear screaming, but I didn't want to say anything to David. How did he know that would work? It turned everything to rust. One of them made it to the train station, but just barely. It was gruesome."

"Wait, she's dead? So only *he's* left." Rainbow got to her feet, unplugged the tabletop record player she kept downstairs for busy weekends during better days and began carrying it upstairs, Lisa locked the door and then followed.

They walked onto Rainbow's balcony and she set it on her Bistro table. She plugged it into the outside outlet that would normally be occupied with Christmas light cords. She went back inside, pulled a record from a sleeve and queued the needle.

"For later, one last time," Rainbow said, and looked over the edge at dozens of White Men, Women, and Children filing into #45 one matchbook at a time.
Lisa looked down in time to see Matthew get out of a Benz she had never seen before, she squeezed Rainbow's hand.

"Oh, I know. He visited this morning and told me to shut it down. I'm only happy he's here tonight to see me, and you, and his mystery tenant from #7 do just that." She squeezed Lisa's hand back.

Inside, the room looked less like normal and more like almost 200 people were missing. Gunnar's wife included. 'Max' came in wearing an eye patch. He strode directly to Gunnar's side and heiled.

"Where is everyone?" Max asked.

"The Triads are all working on a project elsewhere. We...captured the blue eyed rat earlier. He's currently somewhere on Hellgate Bridge, but not for long. It's like they say, 'Man is the most dangerous game'."

"Good. Nothing should keep us from our White Christmas. Speaking of, can we smoke inside tonight since the Biergarten is occupied? Ev's not here yet, is she? Your apartment is a sight to behold, by the way."

"She's tired, pregnancy, and I know it's a boy. She stayed home, but will be here tomorrow. Feel free to light up." David flipped his pack open. A single cigarette stared back, business end up.

"Last one, and it's my Lucky. You want it?" He asked.

"No thank you," Gunnar said as a Probate approached and looked at the pack of Marlboros. "But it looks like people are expecting your weekly community Carton. Go grab it and stop by the Affe's next door, she has meat for us."
'Max' Heiled and headed for the door as calmly as he could.

He ran full speed to the bodega by the C and full speed back to Rainbow's door. She opened it before he could knock.

"He's full of shit! This is going to work!" he could feel himself getting carried away and wanted to vent it before he went back.

"What? About what?" Lisa and Rainbow asked.

"About me, about Evangeline, about where everyone is! He's so full of shit you wouldn't believe it!"

"OK! Good! We're almost there! But not yet." Rainbow's voice had started enthusiastically and ended sternly, like Val's when she meant something.

"Right," he sighed, "he sent me to get the meat though! Hook, line, and sinker! Are the trays set?"

Rainbow nodded and handed David a pair of vinyl gloves, "don't get any on your skin."

They both walked the two trays over.
When David pushed the door open and people saw him with a foil tray and carton of Reds, they cheered, "Max! Max! Max!"

When he moved to reveal Rainbow behind him, the bar went silent.

Gunnar's face flushed scarlet. "WER HAT DEN AFFEN HIER RIENGLASSEN?!"

"Sie bestand darauf, wusste aber nichts," Max said.

"Give me the tray, you dumb NIGGER!" Gunnar ripped it from Rainbow's hands, she felt her glove tear, "get out of OUR BAR!"

Rainbow didn't have to be told twice, she just had to be sure Gunnar had held the tray.
The door closed and Rainbow went back to change gloves and get Lisa. It was time for them to cook a Christmas goose.

'Max' apologized repeatedly, but Gunnar brushed the whole thing off, saying, "Let's get through this rally and then eat and then get to work being good elves for the Welfare Queens and Junkie Monkeys infesting our neighborhood."

Gunnar blew his dog whistle, but Mörder didn't come.
He just sat on the table getting cold waiting for Nazis to take a bite from his bark.

Everyone took their seats after reciting the Pledge of Allegiance and Gunnar began.

"My fellow White Americans, this year has been all the proof a person should need to know that the Negro Race has forgotten its place. From the great Ape, O-Bummer to affirmative action, stealing our jobs and children's education. They steal our daughters and our sons and turn them into gangbangers, wiggers and hoochie mamas! Filthy Race-traitor sluts! But no more! This year we will give our Kinder the White Christmas they deserve. We will prove that there is a magic more powerful than Santa and that it is, WHITE POWER!" The room leapt to its feet in roars and whoops.

Gunnar raised his arms to silence the room, "And we are going to arm at least 100 trees with enough explosives to level whatever building they're in. We may wake up to fire trucks and confusion, but Haarlem belongs to the Dutch, and it's time to make Haarlem White again!"
Everyone raised their arms to 45 degrees to salute Gunnar Erichsen, Grand Dragon.

When everyone broke away for the post-rally feast, David took the bag of explosives and set it by the Robe Check. He watched as hand after hand pressed the edge of the foil pans down against the outer tray. From each he saw clumps of Sterno ooze out onto thumbs and knuckles. He saw the hands mindlessly wipe the wetness on their pants and shirts, if they noticed at all.

He watched as everyone carried plates back to the tables and waited to be led in Grace. Gunnar patted an older woman on the shoulder, and she rose to her feet.

"My name is Catherine. My whole life I have been forced to accept spics, chinks, fags, Democrats and hippies as equal to me. I worry about the sexual predators and drug dealers who are going to kidnap and murder my grandbabies. I am so grateful to our Grand Dragon and his wife for their sacrifice and leadership. Please bow your heads. We must secure the existence of our people and a future for our children. Amen."

Hands and mouths moved on the plates as David knocked three times on the still papered over window and went into the bathroom of the Dog Whistle one final time.

He peed, decided not to flush, but did wash his hands in case he had touched any of the Sterno. He pulled off his eye patch, pulled out his one Green contact lens and dialed Rainbow's Joint from his cell phone.
 "DJ, Could you play Misty for me?"
 "Jesus Christ, David. Your level of bad references really is ageless. Get ready, she's coming," Lisa said.
David remembered being in a bathroom not much larger than this with Odin and Rowan and Cade on the other side almost 1,000 days before. He remembered feeling like nothing could save him, and now he felt like nothing could stop him.
And if it did, Rainbow was there to finish it.
And if not her, Lisa was a foolproof fail safe.

David heard the low murmuring of mass consumption come to a halt. He heard the sound of a song he knew but couldn't make out, then he pulled the Luger out of his pocket and cracked the door open. He heard Rainbow booming in the room.
 "I wanted to come by and say that Y'all's flags don't frighten or disturb me. The overt racism feels, in a way, like a breath of fresh air, *or somethin' like that*. Like my friend Didi

Dunkley used to say before she went missing. Your desire to improve the neighborhood would have helped my friend Beverly and her service dog if it meant better sidewalks for her motorized chair. Not even your flagrant use of nigger bothers me anymore the way it might if you used it in front of someone like Baby Angelo. What bothers me is how none of you tasted the insulin in the meat. *Or the dog in the meat.* You of all people, should have, Gunnar. Little Mörder came through my fence and into my smoker, no problem. But even then, how not one of you noticed missing members at meetings or why my barbecue tastes so unique. *100% American meat.* I told Gunnar when we struck the deal that I wouldn't use anything less. Right Gunnar?"

The room swung, woozily, to him alone at a banquet table, save for Matthew at the far end. He cleared his throat and his phone rang. Cherry Pie by Warrant, filled the room. A few people giggled.

Gunnar raised the phone to his ear, "Ev, hol die Insektenschutztasche."

"Sir," He listened as a Voice he knew, but couldn't place said, "This is America. Speak English."

And then a BlackBerry soared through the air and shattered against the flag draped wall.

"She was your fucking *sister*," David said.

The room tried to digest what he meant.

"A future for our children doesn't mean keep it in the family, you incestophile."

A woman gasped.

"What? Who? What?" Gunnar stammered.

"As your mother burned, she told me. Then I called the Portland Vital Records and found out she wasn't lying. You got your sister pregnant while you posed as a married couple. And now you're going to bomb a city to feel, what? What happens after that? Then who? Who would your nephew-son learn to hate?"

"You killed her!!!" Gunnar exploded.

"You're Goddamn right I did," David, cool and even.

"Die Blauäugige Ratte!" He pulled a gun out.
David pulled Adolf's Luger.

Rainbow pulled her own Luger. "Matthew, I told you last April, I didn't know what you were planning on doing, but I've watched it all unfold. And honestly, Gunnar, some things just are what they are. You, every single one of you, deserve to burn in Hell. And I plan on sending you there."

"Rainbow, don't be stupid. Ein Affe und eine Ratte can't hope to defeat us. We are the rightful heirs to all of this land, and we shouldn't have to see you on it. Get back on a boat and sail back to Africa."

"My name is Judith, you great Holofernes. Rainbow is what God gave my Mama and Daddy to let them know the storm ended with me."
Rainbow pulled a fistful of kitchen matches from her pocket and struck them against the heel of the gun. Puffs of smoke and the sulphury sizzle of every match flashing to life cascaded

through the air, igniting the tablecloths and sleeves of the
Klansmen in a ballet of blue flickers.
She ran, Gunnar fired.
The mirror behind the bar shattered and burst.

David ran, grabbed the bag of C4 and ducked under the yellow
rope that was being pulled taut as Rainbow got ready to yank
as soon as the door was closed.

They heard popping noises out back and new screams of
agony. Gunnar appeared in the hallway and stormed toward
the door.
        David yelled, "You both took my mother from me, I
took your world from you. And God gave *me* a Rainbow."

Judith wound the rope around her forearm and wrist like a
seasoned sailor as she brought the pile of Firs down, blocking
the door.
        She yelled up to Lisa, "flip the record!"

Lisa tossed a Molotov cocktail onto the roof of the Dog
Whistle and watched as it bounced without breaking, then
rolled off the edge and a flourish of orange red light illuminated
the sky.

It was starting to snow. By morning there would be almost 4
inches of dense white powder to bring an early white
Christmas to Harlem.
Lisa lifted the needle, flipped the record, and dropped it again.

She cranked the volume and heard Darlene Love's voice and a symphony of bells drown out the screaming inside number 45.

Christmas filled the night air.

She ran to the street and as Lisa, David, and Rainbow sang at the top of their lungs,
> ***THE CHURCH BELLS IN TOWN***
> ***ARE RINGING A SONG***
> ***FULL OF HAPPY SOUNDS***
> ***BABY, PLEASE COME HOME***

They watched the bar burn as fire trucks arrived but weren't able to access the hydrants because they were blocked by 1300 Firs.

Rainbow said she thought the people inside had planned on donating to neighborhood families.

David said he found the duffel bag when he ran in to see if anyone was inside, but back out when he saw everyone was dead from what seemed like an explosion, "I thought it might have been batteries? I know batteries are bad in a fire. I learned the hard way as a kid on the farm."

Lisa said her ex-husband had invited her here for a meeting that he wouldn't tell her about. He had just given her this matchbook and told her to come on the 19th at 9 to see what was new in the neighborhood. "We used to own the apartments down the way. When we were married. He got them all in the divorce. And this bar."

"Did you two get in a fight one morning up the street after some guy died in one of those apartments? You two I mean." The investigator pointed to Lisa and Rainbow.

"We did. It turns out we were on the same side, just judged wrong and out of pocket, Lisa has had dinner with me every month since the divorce. Neither of us will ever forget Jim Richards' death," Rainbow covered.

The fire burned evenly and didn't damage any surrounding property. Fire Marshals would later state that it was in large part due to the heavy and immediate snowfall at the time of the fire.

"Mother Nature did what our Men couldn't," one investigator said.

Postlude

1/20/2009 12:07 pm
A New Birth of Freedom

*"What is required of us now is a new era of responsibility—
a recognition, on the part of every American."*
~President Obama, *2009 Inauguration Address*

On January 20th, 2009, Barack Hussein Obama
became President of the United States. The in-person
attendance record was the highest ever in Washington, DC.
Globally, it was one of the most watched events of all time. His
wife, First Lady Michelle Obama, their two daughters Sasha
and Malia and Barack all lived at 1600 Pennsylvania Avenue for
four years without scandal.

Though President Obama won 69 million votes in 2008,
anti-Black violence and rhetoric, along with an economy that
lambasted his every move, meant only 65 million people voted
him handily into his second term.

In the second four years of Obama's residency at 1600
Pennsylvania, a scandal arose when Michelle decided to visit
Target without gaining proper security clearance first.

A brief letter from the author to you:

First of all, thank you. I hope, from the bottom of everything inside of me, that this story changed you the way it changed me. I sat down one afternoon in late July to see if a simple idea in my mind could hold water; What if a little old lady was pushed too far by the skinheads next door? I wrote, by hand, the first page of the first six chapters, and thought it might work. Over the next three weeks I sat almost around the clock, thinking, reasoning, and deciding why this story was compelling beyond the promise of the unthinkable. Pen after pen died as I took notes on real acts of terror against Black Americans in the last 100 years on a deeper level than I ever had.

> To My Avery who would tell me when it was time to put the pen down and eat. Without you my life would lack purpose and meaning. Of every adventure I've ever been on, ours is my very favorite. I love you.

We'd go to meat-heavy restaurants and I would listen to other diners describe their food.

After I realized the Jorgensens were Judith's boiling point, Avery and I went on a mushroom trip with friends and ate a giant platter of Greek meat. I contemplated veganism or giving up the book.

The Morality Play inside the story was very straightforward to me. It was a way to demonstrate my views on God.

Sure, it's not a new idea considering the concept, but my idea
of who God is shaped the harshest justices in the story.
This is who God is to me:
She's a little old lady at a kitchen table doing her checkbook for
the month.
Putting her Social Security and Pension checks down in Black,
putting her mortgage and medicine down in Red. Playing *the
money game.*
But she; like every other little old lady, knows that there are
random events tied to money as well.
A child's birthday present, money from a friend for Christmas,
$20 you find in the bottom of an ATM and keep your mouth
shut about.
The ledger of life is, by definition, filled with Blacks and Reds.
It doesn't factor in these events.
That's where whatever pen is closest comes, literally, in hand.
Sometimes blue or green or purple.
Sometimes from a bank or hotel or taken by accident from a
waitress at a barbecue joint.
A rainbow of entries across a lifetime of negative-positives and
positive-negatives. And balance. And hopefully enough to
cover your bills at the end of it all.

And now we're here.
At the other end of the rainbow,
I hope you found you have a heart of gold.
My dream is that this book is taught in high schools
nationwide until the year 2100.

Nothing in this story was premeditated, yet when I would Google to see if I was right, Divine Intervention would tell me to keep going.

August 4th, 1944 was sunny and warm in both Amsterdams. Yet my reason for "making it Rainbow's birthday" was as simple as it's the day my grandmother was born.

4 inches of snow did rapidly fall on December 19th, 2008 in Harlem but my reason for ending the book then is, it is my favorite date, my grandparents anniversary.

To Katie, Kevin, Susan, Jeremy, Jessica, Courtney, Mark, Matthew, Devin, Eliana, Traci, Angela, Jolie, Sarah, and Melissa, thank you for being rainbows before anyone knew what it meant. Without you, this little book would have had no budget or chance to shine.

But now what?
Well, tell a friend to visit Rainbow's Joint and see if they make her wear gloves.
Vote. If you're still living in a democracy.
Say good morning to your neighbor and hold the door for people at the store.
Try to be a rainbow.

James Alejandro-Sueling-Loons, 7.20.2023-8.16.2023

www.ingramcontent.com/pod-product-compliance
Lightning Source LLC
Chambersburg PA
CBHW030620310726